A Beth-Hill Novel:
The Shadows Trilogy,
Book 2: Lost in Shadows

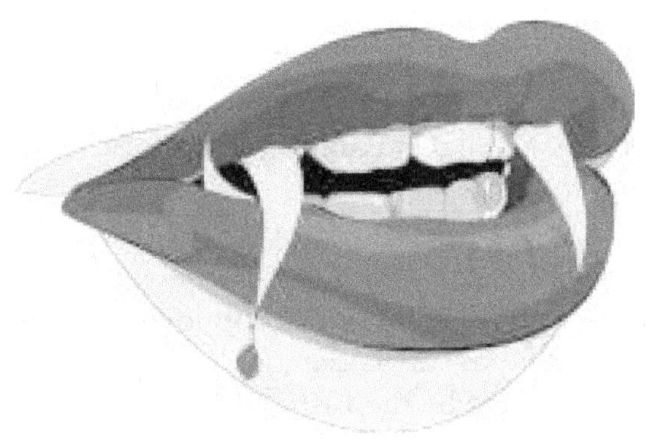

By Jennifer St. Clair

Writers Exchange E-Publishing

http://www.writers-exchange.com

For my family

Chapter 1

"He is alive, and I want you to bring him to me." Terrin did not turn from the window to face the figure standing beside the door.

"But I saw him die, my lord. How can Nicodemus be alive?" The voice was rough with suspicion. "It has to be a trick."

"It is no trick. Skade holds his spirit in a mirror; he's trapped in there with her cursed spells. When I..." Terrin glanced down at his clenched hands and felt the smooth, unbroken flow of his spell between them. "When I liberated my sons from Iomar, I found him. She's been hiding him in plain sight all this time."

"I don't like it," the dark figure muttered. "I don't like going into Iomar. You know she has wards set against us, don't you? It hurts when I go there."

"The wards are nothing," Terrin growled. "I want you to bring me Nicodemus. I don't care who you have to kill to get him out of that mirror. Do you understand what I mean?"

"Yes, my lord."

"I'd do it myself, but she knows me. She doesn't know you. Go to Iomar. Find Nicodemus, and bring him back in this." He held out a small black velvet bag. "Disguise yourself as one of her servants, perhaps. She has enough of them in that cursed castle."

A gloved hand took the bag from Terrin's fingers and opened it. The dark figure shook a delicate crystal pendant out on the palm of his hand and held it up so it sparkled in the moonlight.

"Trap him in this? How?"

"Blood, you fool. How do you think she put him in that mirror in the first place?" Terrin pulled on the spell and felt his son jerk in his sleep. He smiled. "Kill as many of her servants as you need to; just bring him back."

"Yes, my lord." The dark figure slipped the pendant back into the bag. His form seemed to shimmer in the darkness for a moment, then he stepped out of the shadows and bowed to Terrin, no longer gloved; no longer shadowed.

"I could go as Michael."

Terrin's lips twitched. "And blame him again for something he had no part in? The idea has its merits, I'll admit. She will be furious if she thinks her son has returned to rescue his friend."

"So?"

"Do we know where he is?" Terrin asked, turning back to stare out the window. "We might need to...ensure his cooperation."

"Once we have Nicodemus, we can find out."

"Then proceed."

Chapter 2

Skade had given up, but Nicodemus had not. He spent hours trying to slip past Terrin's spells; hours he could have spent alone in the gray featureless confines of the mirror as he had for so many years.

She had let him keep his name, but the memories were gone again. He was glad of that; they would have only distracted him and gotten in the way. Without them, he could concentrate on finding Alban and the vampire. So far, his luck had been marginal at best.

Skade's beads were the only link he had to the castle, but Terrin's spells had so far prevented him from linking up to them again. He had managed to see into the throne room where he had last seen Alban and the vampire, but both were gone and Terrin had not returned.

"Have you found them yet?" Skade's voice pulled him away from Leysan and back to the mirror. Nicodemus blinked at her.

"Found them?" *Had she known of his search all along?*

"Espen tells me we have no true cause to attack Leysan unless we know the vampire and Alban are alive." There were lines on Skade's forehead that had not been there before, and dark circles under her eyes. "I know you're still looking for them, Mir...Nicodemus."

Even though his name no longer caused him pain, he could not help but flinch. "I won't give up." He said this as if he expected her to punish him.

She favored him with a small smile. "I don't expect you to. In fact, I want you to find them."

"I want to find them too," the Ghost said softly.

Skade gave him an appraising glance. "You're not blaming yourself, are you? It wasn't your fault."

"It was my mirror." He closed his eyes and turned away from her, remembering the pain of Terrin's spell.

"It wasn't your fault." Skade put one hand on the mirror. "Nicodemus, look at me."

He opened his eyes. Her face blurred until he blinked the tears away.

"It wasn't your fault."

"I know." He hit his side of the mirror in frustration and watched the spells ripple across the glass. "But it was my mirror. I can't help but feel responsible."

Skade smiled. "If anyone should feel responsible, it should be me. This is my castle. I told them they were safe here."

Nicodemus shrugged.

"You have changed." Skade stared at him. "For the better, I think. Before, you wouldn't have felt responsible for anything."

She had honored his request not to remember anything from his former life, but sometimes he wished she had refused. He knew from his reactions to the memories that they had not been good ones, but they were still a part of him, of his identity.

"I feel responsible now, my lady." He had lost most of his fear of her since Alban and the vampire vanished. "And I won't stop until I find them."

"And if they're dead?" Skade spoke the question neither of them wanted to voice.

"Then I will help you make Terrin pay."

Skade nodded, satisfied. "I don't want you to risk your life to find out if they're alive, Nicodemus. Do you understand me?"

He would risk his soul if he had a chance to free them, but he would not tell her that. He had a feeling she already knew.

Chapter 3

The vampire lay in darkness, pain coloring his vision red. He could not move; could not protect himself from the rats that crept up to sniff his flesh. His entire body felt like it was on fire and movement would be agony.

After a little while, he managed to twitch a finger, and felt something smooth against the palm of his hand. He didn't realize what it was until much later, after he lifted his arm and curled his hand on his chest.

Skade's bracelet glittered on his arm. He did not remember picking it up before Terrin banished him to the dungeons. He certainly didn't remember slipping it on his arm.

He concentrated on the bracelet for a while, slowly curling his fingers until he managed to push it far enough forward to touch the row of red beads. Nothing happened, but he was not really disappointed. He had felt Terrin seal the castle against outside spells. Obviously Skade could not get through, but could he help her along a little?

He had his name back now, after all. The repercussions of that still shuddered through his mind. A name equaled power, and power meant he might be able to get a message to Skade. He just hoped she wouldn't give up.

He concentrated on the beads. He thought he had sensed a presence in them before, but it was gone now. The beads were only beads, powerful in their own right, but not powerful enough to free him or Alban.

A rustling sound near his ear told him the rats were still trying to decide if he would taste good or not. The vampire wished he could drink their blood, but he knew it would not help him. And he was too weak to catch them, now. Terrin had seen to that.

He ignored the rats and concentrated on Skade's beads again, struggling past the numbing weakness to find any shred of power he could utilize. He found nothing. No power, no strength. He felt a tear slip down the side of his face.

One of the rats licked it off.

The vampire shuddered and closed his eyes as the rat clambered over his face, its cold greasy feet leaving a faint unpleasantness across his skin. The rat halted on his chest and crouched over Skade's bracelet. The vampire tried to shoo it away, but it was not fazed by the weak twitching of his hand.

He felt a tug on the bracelet, as the rat worked at the string that knotted the beads together. Panic bloomed in the vampire's chest. Without the bracelet, he had no hope. Without the bracelet, he might as well let the rats eat him.

The rat ignored his frantic attempts to scare it away. It nipped his flesh more than once, but the vampire saw no blood from the wounds.

When the first thread parted beneath the rat's sharp teeth, the vampire felt something course through his body and lodge in his heart. He gasped.

The rat glanced back at him, then returned to its work. Its elongated face seemed to be bathed in bloody red, as if the beads had begun to glow again, but they remained dark and silent, their beauty marred by the rat's saliva.

The vampire felt the last thread part. The beads fell away from his wrist and onto his chest. One rolled off into the rotted straw, but the others remained. Skade's bracelet was well made.

The rat took one of the beads into its mouth and dragged them back the way it had come. The vampire closed his eyes again, expecting to feel the damp feet press against his eyes, but the rat didn't seem to be in a hurry to climb back down to the floor.

He cracked open one eye just as the rat's claws scraped across his cheekbone. Pain flared through his head. He opened his mouth to scream.

One of the beads at the very end of the string fell into his open mouth. It lay there for a moment against his tongue, cold and alien, then slowly warmed. The familiar taste of blood filled his mouth. He swallowed convulsively, and the bead slid down his throat, dissolving as it went.

He almost choked as blessed warmth crept through his veins, stirring both power and pain. The rat, oblivious, struggled to pull the strand of beads away.

The vampire closed his mouth and locked his teeth around the string. The beads continued to dissolve, giving him much-needed nourishment. He didn't understand how they could be blood and beads at the same time, but he wasn't about to question his good fortune.

After a minute, he found he had enough strength to sit up and wrest the rest of the strand of beads from the rat, who scurried into a large hole in the wall. The vampire stared at it for a moment, then leaned back against the seeping wall and clenched his fingers around the beads. He had two choices. If the rest of the beads worked the same as the ones that had already dissolved, he could use them all now and then see if he had enough strength to escape. His other choice would be to stay half-starved for as long as he could, and hope for rescue.

Neither choice seemed very promising.

One of the rats slipped out of the hole, and a large piece of the wall fell away under its scrabbling paws. The vampire stared. It was possible--barely--that the rats might know a way out of the castle that Terrin had not blocked. He crawled across the cell, cradling the beads against his chest with one hand, and watched the rats scatter away.

When he groped inside the hole, he felt only emptiness as far as he could reach. The darkness beyond the hole smelled like rotting meat, but he felt a faint breeze slide across his skin.

A breeze might mean a way out. And he had no other options but to try.

He swallowed all but three of the remaining beads, waited for the strength to trickle into his body, and slowly began to work at the crumbling hole.

It didn't take him very long to widen it enough to squeeze through, but he stuck his head through first to make sure he would not fall down some forgotten shaft and break every bone in his body. The rats' thoroughfare seemed to be a gap between cells; a narrow passageway that led into darkness.

He scraped his skin raw wriggling through the widened hole, but he did fit into the passageway and crawled on hands and knees towards the source of the faint breeze.

He tried to ignore the muck squishing up between his fingers and the rats that scurried out of his way. He had to focus on freedom.

Or failing that, somehow getting a message to Skade that he was not dead.

Chapter 4

"Espen said you should drink this." A small, pale hand held an even smaller cup to his lips and Teluride wrinkled his nose at the smell.

"What is it?" His voice had not improved, but he had managed to stay awake for four straight hours before sleeping for twelve.

Zaira shrugged. He remembered her name more easily than anyone else's; no one else looked quite like her.

"Medicine, probably. Do you want me to help you drink it?"

Teluride managed to choke down the vile brew, but it left a pleasantly warm sensation in his stomach. He sighed and lay back against the pillows, weary even though he had just awakened.

"How are you feeling today?" Zaira asked.

Teluride considered her question carefully. He had no reference as to how badly he had felt before he lost his memory, but each day brought a tiny bit of improvement to the whole.

"I think I feel better. I just wish..." He sighed and closed his eyes. "I wish I knew if I will ever get my memory back."

Zaira bit her lip and glanced towards the door. "I could tell you if you ask me."

"You could? How?"

"I dream the future. If you ask me, I will know."

Teluride stared at her; suddenly not sure he wanted to know. If he knew he'd never recover his memory, would he try as hard to struggle past the weakness that plagued his body and soul?

"I'll...think about it," he whispered.

Zaira nodded solemnly. "I thought you would. Espen will be here soon; do you need anything before she comes?"

"Just your company would be fine," Teluride whispered.

"Then I'll stay right here with you."

He drifted away with the comfort that he was not alone.

Later, when he opened his eyes, Zaira was gone and Espen sat beside him, idly flipping through a tattered paperback book. She set the book aside when he opened his eyes.

"How do you feel?"

If anything, he felt worse. He struggled not to give in to the nausea rolling in his stomach, but he could not hold it back. He rolled over and vomited all over Espen's clean white sheets.

"I'm sorry..."

"Don't apologize." Espen ignored the mess and concentrated on Teluride. She laid her hands against his temples and closed her eyes. A moment later they were open again and a frown marred her dark features.

"Well, that didn't work."

Teluride could hardly keep his eyes open. "What?"

"I mixed up something that should have helped your memory return, but it didn't work. At all."

"The room's spinning," Teluride whispered. He watched it for a little while, too dazed to get dizzy.

Espen worked over him in silence for a long time, until she made him to drink something else that looked like water but burned like fire going down. He choked and coughed, but she forced him to swallow.

Instantly, the nausea vanished. The room settled down and stayed in place. He cautiously opened his eyes.

Espen settled back in the chair again and frowned at him. "I have a feeling you weren't allergic to my magic before Terrin did this to you."

"Allergic?"

"I've never seen someone have such a strong reaction to my potions," Espen said. "So yes, allergic. I'll have to be careful from now on."

"What was in that last one?" Teluride asked. He almost felt clear-headed for the first time since he awoke back in Leysan with his memory missing.

Espen glanced at him, an odd look on her face. "Water."

"Just water?"

She nodded. "Just water."

Teluride blinked. "Can I have some more?" Even his voice sounded better.

Espen put one hand on his forehead, frowned, and then shook her head. "I don't see why not. I'll be right back."

He drank three glasses of water before sleep stole him away again, but this time the darkness wasn't so deep.

Chapter 5

Something surged through Nicodemus' mirror, sending ripples of power across the bars of Skade's spell. He stood and watched as the energy fractured one bar and destroyed another, but made no move to escape.

The energy had come from Leysan. He was almost sure of it. He sent a thin tendril of awareness back across the path it had taken, and found a tiny crack in Terrin's wards where it had escaped. He had no idea who had sent the spell to find him; or if it was truly a spell, but he managed to slip an even tinier tendril of himself past Terrin's wards and inside the castle.

Cold numbed his soul and sucked all warmth away from his insubstantial body. Nicodemus froze in place, staring at something only he could see; a flat, featureless room that housed an iron cage. And inside that iron cage...

He stepped closer to it and stared down at Alban's slack features. He could see the spell that bound him as clearly as the bars that surrounded him, but he could not remove the spell without destroying Alban's mind, or worse.

It only took him a moment to realize what Terrin had done to his son. Was the vampire dead, then? Had Terrin killed him?

Nicodemus closed his eyes and send out feelers into the castle around him, skirting spells that would set off alarms and giving Terrin's awareness a wide berth. He found the bodies of the Council lying where they had fallen, and marveled at Terrin's madness for a moment before moving downward, into the dungeons.

It took him three hours to find his only clue; a bead from the bracelet Skade had given Alban, nestled in a pile of rotting straw in a tiny dungeon cell.

He tried to pass through the hole in the cell's wall, but he had already stretched himself too thin, and the cracked spell binding him to the mirror itched at the edge of his mind and he could not concentrate on staying in Leysan.

Skade would not be happy with him if he could not return to Iomar. He released the pieces of himself, opened his eyes, and found himself back in his prison with the broken shards of Skade's spell sparking in his ears.

He stood, took one step forward, and accidentally touched the broken spell.

Pain flared up his arm and sent him crashing to the featureless floor. He gasped and dragged himself away from the front of the mirror.

Through the wavering glass, Nicodemus saw Skade's door open. He struggled to his feet, intending to tell her what he had found, but one of her young maids stepped through the door instead.

And behind her, a tall red-haired man who looked familiar, but Nicodemus had a sinking feeling his identity was buried under the memories he did not want to face.

The man glanced around, evidently looking for Skade, then pushed the girl towards the mirror.

"Nicodemus?" His voice was rough and grating on the Ghost's ears.

"M-my Queen will..."

The man slapped the girl to quiet her and she fell against the mirror, cracking the spells even further. A thin smear of blood glowed against the glass before the man pulled her away.

"Nicodemus!" The man stepped up to the mirror and peered into the glass as if he could see to the other side.

Even though the Ghost knew he could not, he stepped back anyway. *Where was Skade?*

The man growled something and pulled the girl up to face the mirror. He drew a knife from his belt, showed it to her, then clamped one hand over her mouth, forcing her to raise her head.

Before Nicodemus realized what he planned, the man drew the knife across the girl's taut throat. Blood sprayed on the mirror and soaked through to the prison on the other side.

"Skade?" the Ghost whispered, frozen. He stared in disbelief as the man tossed the dying girl down and withdrew a delicate crystal pendant from a small velvet bag. He smeared some of the girl's blood on the pendant, and Nicodemus felt a strange pulling sensation wrap around his middle and tug him towards the remnants of Skade's spell.

He tried again, "Skade!" This time his voice rang out and reached the man's ears.

He grimaced. "I don't think she can help you right now, Nicodemus. Your witch is a bit distracted."

The tugging sensation strengthened. Nicodemus tried to resist, but he had nothing to hold onto, and the girl's blood made everything slippery and wet.

When he passed through the spells, they sent jolts of pain through his body and almost cast him into darkness. He had no chance to relish freedom.

He closed his eyes as a ripple of pain shot through his body, and when he opened them again, he looked out at Skade's room from the skewed perspective of the crystal pendant.

"Someone wants to see you," the man growled, and slipped the pendant back into the velvet bag.

As darkness covered him, the Ghost could only think of Alban, lying alone and unresponsive inside that iron cage and the single red bead he had found in that stinking cell. He tried to reach out and leave Skade some sort of message, but he could not feel the spells anymore, and the crystal trapped him much more effectively than any of Skade's spells ever had.

Again, he wished Skade had not obeyed his wishes and blocked his memory again. With memory intact, he would know who the man was and why he was willing to kill an innocent girl to take him away from Iomar. With his memories, he thought he might be able to attempt an escape, but without them he knew nothing and couldn't plan a thing.

What would Skade say when she found him gone?

Chapter 6

"Damn." Skade watched as two of her personal guards removed the maid's body from her room, and stared at the bloody mirror. "Damn, damn, and double damn."

"My lady?" one of the guards hesitated in the doorway. "My lady, we found out where he came in."

She had neglected both her duties and her wards. She had assumed herself to be untouchable, even after Terrin's flamboyant disregard of her power. Nicodemus had regained his memory, if only for a moment before she honored his wishes and buried it again. She should have realized they would still be watching her, even after all these years.

The question she had to ask, though; the question that rose to the forefront of her mind and wouldn't leave her alone haunted her until she faced the mirror and spoke it aloud.

"Did you go with them willingly, Nicodemus?"

The mirror remained dark and unresponsive, the spells broken. Skade put her hand to the glass and cursed them loud and long. It didn't really make her feel any better, but at least the ends of her hair stopped sparking with unused magic.

In an eerie echo of that desperate search ten years ago, she sent out her guards to comb the countryside for any sign of the Ghost or his kidnapper. They returned empty-handed, of course. Skade was not surprised.

She drew on her magic, on the power that coursed through the stones of Iomar, and directed it in a search for her missing Ghost. After that failed, she slipped down into the little-used dungeons, past the worried faces of her staff and the stiff ones of her guards; past those who remembered what had happened in Iomar ten years ago and past those who did not.

The scandal, if that was a good enough name for it, had not been known in every circle. Oh, everyone knew something had happened, but only a handful of people knew the details. Skade knew. Her son had been one of the instigators of it all. Espen knew; the scandal had touched her band of Healers far too intimately.

Terrin knew, and what remained of the others who had plotted against the very soul of the Seven Kingdoms.

Skade slipped past the cleaner cells and down into the lower levels where no one had gone for many years. As far as she knew, she was the only one in Iomar who knew how to get past the spells that glowed across the door to the lower levels, and the dust on the floor told her no one had tried to break through since she had set the spells ten years before.

She opened the door, releasing dry musty air, then hurried down the row of crumbling cells to the very last one. These spells were more difficult to break, but they recognized their maker.

When she opened that door, she relaxed, even though she knew no one had dared to try and find him.

Nicodemus' body lay undisturbed on a small bed, covered by a dusty quilt and an equally dusty sheet. His body was the only thing free of dust; she had given him that dignity, at least.

He seemed so young, lying there. The spell kept him alive but soulless; she had taken his essence and trapped it in the mirror and that was what she had been interacting with since she locked him in here. Seeing him as flesh and blood after so long came as a shock.

"You're still here." She crossed to the mirror leaning against one wall and regarded her reflection. "You're still here, so they haven't gotten that far yet. Let's see if we can figure out who stole you from me, Nicodemus."

She angled the mirror so it showed the body in the bed, then took out a small penknife and pricked her finger with the blade. She smeared her blood on the mirror, and then did the same with Nicodemus' blood.

Their blood sizzled a bit when it touched, but that was from the sickness that would have killed him, nothing else.

"Who stole you, Nicodemus? Tell me who took you away from me."

The mirror shimmered and the blood slowly vanished from the glass. In its place, Skade saw her room, a frightened maid, and a face she thought she would never see again.

She gasped, swayed, and caught herself against the mirror's glass, right over the face of her son.

Chapter 7

The vampire found the first sleepers when he slipped in the muck and slid a hundred feet down a slope. The passageway opened up into a large room that had what looked like hundreds of bodies lying in beds that stretched as far as the room was wide.

He hesitated at the mouth of the passageway and waited for them to wake up and sound the alarm, but they slept on, their chests rising and falling regularly.

Only when he approached them did he start to sense something wrong.

Most of the bodies were Iomarian, with the distinctive red hair and pale skin of Skade's people. Some of them looked to be from Leysan, or perhaps Glinyeu. Eighteen were children, the youngest probably three or four. Twenty beds lay empty. There were eighty-five people in all.

Each body glowed with a subtle blue glow that he surmised was the spell keeping them asleep. Skade's magic was blue, but what would they be doing in Leysan and not Iomar? And why would she keep them asleep?

He realized she had to have a very good reason to keep them here, and wondered if she would be forced to keep him here with them now that he had seen the sleepers.

Had he destroyed his chance of getting back to Iomar?

A mirror leaned against one wall, and the vampire studied his dusty reflection for a moment. He tried to wipe the worst of the muck away, but he couldn't scrub it off his skin without something clean to scrub with.

He had no idea how to find Skade using the mirror, or even if he would be able to, but he knew he had to try. With shaking fingers, he placed the next to last bead in his mouth and let it dissolve on his tongue. Even though his body cried out for blood, he rubbed a bit of it on the mirror before swallowing.

"Skade?" His voice cracked and he felt tears gather in his eyes. "Skade, can you hear me?"

Instead of Skade, another face appeared; one he did not recognize. This woman's face was dark, darker than anything he had ever seen, but her eyes were kind. She wore her hair in tiny little braids all around her head and the beads on the ends of the braids clinked when she moved.

"Oh my." Her voice soothed him, as warm as Skade's bed. "Oh my. Skade will be so glad you're alive. Wait right there; I have to get to a larger mirror."

The vampire sank to his knees. "You know Skade?"

The woman nodded. "I'm Espen. I don't believe we've met."

Espen was the witch who had Terrin's Dreamer, Zaira, and who had taken Teluride away to be healed. The vampire felt something loosen in his chest. The dam of tears broke and spilled over his cheeks.

A moment later, he felt a warm hand on his shoulder. Espen stepped through the mirror and gathered him up into her arms He sobbed against her chest.

"Shhh," She rocked him back and forth on the floor, unmindful of the filth that covered him even though he tried to pull away. "Shhh. You're safe now. You can come back with me and keep Zaira company."

That sounded heavenly, but that also meant he would abandon Alban to their father's whims. He raised his head.

"I don't want to leave my brother here."

"We won't leave him here for long. We'll find him. I promise."

"My...my father made me do it," the vampire whispered, close to collapse. He struggled to push away the darkness, but utter exhaustion left him with nothing more to bargain with. "He made me do it."

Espen stood with him still in her arms. "What did he make you do?"

"Alban was dead." The vampire thought it important that he tell her now, just in case she didn't want to bring him with her after she found out what he had done. "Alban was dead, and my father made me bring him back to life." He closed his eyes, not wanting to see the expression on her face.

"Oh, you poor child."

He felt something shimmer over his body when Espen carried him through the mirror, but the blackness was too strong for him to take notice of it.

"Sleep now," he heard her say. "I'll contact Skade and let her know you're all right."

He tried to struggle out of darkness to wait and hear Skade's verdict, but it pulled him downward, deeper and deeper until he could neither hear nor see.

He let it take him, and slept too deeply for dreams.

Chapter 8

When Skade returned to her room, the last maid had just left and the mirror showed her failure clearly. She did not look at her reflection, but passed it by and sank into a chair.

She was so cold. Cold in mind, heart, body, and soul. She didn't know which way to turn now that Nicodemus was gone. She had relied on him for too long.

She leaned back in her chair and rubbed her hands together, trying to shake the numbness from her fingers. She didn't realize she was crying until a hot tear plopped on her hand.

Skade wiped her eyes and sat for a moment, desperately trying to regain her composure. It would not do to let anyone see her like this; they might find a way to use it against her.

After she dried her tears, she stood and slowly made her way to the mirror again. She had not attempted to contact her son since he was exiled ten years ago. She had locked the memories away, but his face in the mirror as he slit the poor maid's throat had broken them free.

Her hand shook when she placed it against the cold glass of the mirror. She cleared her throat. "Michael. Show me my son."

The mirror glowed softly at her request, and she absently removed the broken spell that had kept Nicodemus inside his prison as she waited. She saw a spot of blood on the rug that her maid had missed, and her eyes filled with tears once more.

Why had he returned? What did he expect Nicodemus to do for him, as a ghost? She had blocked his memories, but she had no doubt her block could be removed. But to what purpose? No one had found a cure for the sickness that they had wrought, and it had been ten years.

She realized she should contact Espen and tell her what had happened, but she didn't want to endure another lecture. Losing Alban and the vampire had been bad enough. Losing Nicodemus...Espen would be furious.

The mirror glowed. What was taking it so long? Michael had been exiled, not sentenced to death.

She half-wished he had died in the intervening years, but he was very obviously alive.

Finally, the mirror showed a wavering scene, the inside of what looked to be a small house. Skade carefully kept the connection and sharpened the picture; it was night wherever her son lived now.

How had he gotten past the spells involved in his exile? He shouldn't have been able to set foot in Iomar, and yet he had walked right into her room and stolen Nicodemus from under her nose.

As she watched a door opened and a dark figure slipped into the room. He glanced at the mirror she had connected to, but he saw only his reflection.

Skade saw the faint traceries of wards around the open door, and wondered why the alarms had not gone off.

"Show me my son," she instructed the mirror, but it stayed fixed on the shadowy room. Did he only have one mirror in his house? Frustrated, she tried to follow the dark figure as it passed through the doorway to the next room, but she couldn't find another reflective surface anywhere.

She growled, fashioned a portal between the two mirrors, and stepped into cool darkness. Strange furniture lurked at the edges of the room. The mirror she had passed through reflected moonlight from the nearby window, but didn't shed enough light to tell Skade where she was.

On silent feet, she followed the dark figure, but it had vanished into another room. She stood in the middle of the hallway for a moment and sent a tiny sliver of power through each and every door, trying to find the one her son slept behind.

One of the doors led to a kitchen. Skade peeked inside and saw a confusing array of appliances, but no servants. She shook her head.

The next door led to what looked to be a bathroom, all gleaming white and ugly. Not a single piece of tile was to be found, and all the soaps and shampoos were not handmade.

The next door led to an unused bedroom, plain and simple, with a rug on the floor and a quilt on the bed. Skade stared at a picture hanging on the wall for a moment; it resembled Iomar in both looks and color.

She continued to explore the house. Once she thought she heard a thump from upstairs, but when she crept up the stairs to investigate, she found no sign of the intruder.

What if the dark figure hadn't been an intruder after all? What if Michael's house was their headquarters? Would she find Nicodemus here in this strange place?

She heard another thump behind one of the closed doors, and a child's voice cried out. The wards screamed in protest as something large slipped through them.

The entire house shook. Skade grabbed the banister to keep from falling down the stairs. A vase full of bright yellow daisies toppled off a table and smashed on the floor.

A door opened down the hall and her son appeared in the doorway. He didn't notice her yet; the hallway was too dark. He hurried to the door closest to the stairs, opened it, and flicked on a light inside the room.

It was a child's room with pink walls and a garden of flowers painted across the ceiling. A scruffy teddy bear lay on the floor at Michael's feet, and he absently picked it up as he stepped inside the room.

"Enapay?"

The wards shrieked until Michael noticed and silenced them with a twitch of his fingers. The house stopped shaking, and something downstairs fell over with a loud crash. Skade slowly got to her feet.

She was curiously reluctant to show herself to him, but she couldn't stand in the hallway forever.

"Enapay?" he asked again. She watched as he moved around, as if the child--his child?--would magically appear.

A sudden breeze blew a mobile hanging from an antique light, and Skade moved into the lighted doorway just as Michael leaned out over the open window.

A horrible suspicion began to sprout in Skade's mind. Michael had been asleep; that much was obvious. He wore a tattered short-sleeved shirt and a pair of cut-off pants and his hair stuck up in odd angles all across his head.

He didn't act like he had just been to Iomar and stolen Nicodemus, but Skade had seen his face in the mirror!

But had it been his face? As he turned away from the window, still searching the room for any sign of the child, she mentally compared what she had seen in the mirror to what she saw now before her.

The Michael in the mirror had not aged. This Michael, her son, looked older, more careworn, and slightly fragile around the edges. This Michael--and she would bet her life on it--had not been to Iomar.

She had been tricked.

Chapter 9

Before she could move away from the door, Michael saw her and froze. Skade saw a series of emotions run across his face, from abject terror to hate.

"You?" His voice was harsh, disbelieving. "Where is my daughter?"

Skade's heart gave a strange little flip. His daughter. She had a granddaughter.

"I didn't take her," she said. "I followed someone here, but I didn't get here in time."

"Where is my daughter?" He flung something invisible at her, his eyes bright with tears. She caught it easily and let it subside. She did not want to quarrel with him if he had not been involved in Nicodemus' disappearance.

If he wasn't involved in Nicodemus' disappearance, then had he been involved in... She shut that thought out of her mind. He had been tried, convicted, and exiled. She shouldn't even be talking to him. But the thought remained. If someone had taken on Michael's face to steal Nicodemus, then they could have easily done so before. The murders...the subsequent disappearances...

Skade stared at her son. "Michael, were you involved in Nicodemus' disappearance?"

He flinched back as if she had struck him. "Nicodemus has been dead for years."

"Nicodemus has been my Mirror for ten years," Skade said softly. "He lives, still, but he would die if I released him back into his body."

Michael closed his eyes, the anger draining away. "It's been a lot longer than ten years here."

"Where are we?" Skade asked.

"Far away from Iomar," Michael said. "Where is my daughter?"

Skade saw a picture frame sitting on a painted table beside the messy bed. She stepped past her son and picked it up. A young family stared back at her; Michael was obvious and easy to pick out. The woman beside him, with her short-cropped hair and clear skin, had given her brown eyes to the child between them.

Her granddaughter. The child had curly red hair and a gap toothed grin. She wore a dark blue dress in the picture and someone had tried to tame those curls into two braids.

"What is her name?"

"Enapay." Michael's voice softened. "I...I didn't tell Sarah it was your mother's name."

"My mother would have been honored," Skade said honestly. "Is Sarah...your wife?"

"She's not here. She had to go to England to..." Michael gave a soft cry of despair. "Why am I telling you this? Where is my daughter?"

"Michael, if I ask you one question, will you answer it honestly?" Skade stared at him, the coldness now lodged in her heart. What if she had wronged him ten years ago? How could she ever forgive herself? How could he ever forgive her?

"Will you give me my daughter back if I answer your question?" Michael asked. He clutched the teddy bear to his chest, but seemed to have forgotten it was there.

"I don't have her, but I think I know who does." Skade took a deep breath. "Michael, tell me the truth. Were you guilty?"

He stared at her for a long moment, then turned away. She waited. After one hundred heartbeats, she opened her mouth to ask again.

"I am guilty of naivety, nothing more," he whispered. Every word seemed to be torn from his throat. "I am guilty of believing lies and looking away when I should have been paying more attention."

"You didn't create the spell." Skade heard her voice crack. "You didn't do any of the experiments. You weren't the one who nearly destroyed the Seven Kingdoms."

Michael's shoulders stiffened. "No. I was the one who got blamed for all of it."

The enormity of what he claimed shook her very soul. Skade sank down on Enapay's bed and stared at the face in the picture.

"Michael, I...I don't know what to say."

"Tell me you'll bring my daughter back," Michael whispered.

"I didn't take her."

"You said you know who did." He did not turn around.

"Yes, I think I do. But I'm not sure why."

A piece of paper fluttered through the open window and landed at Michael's feet. His reaction was extraordinary. He jumped away from it and stared down at it, frozen in fear.

Skade stared at him for a moment. What had happened to him in the years he had been gone? He had obviously not left the magic behind; but why would he be frightened of a folded piece of paper? When she reached down to pick it up, his breath hissed between his teeth, but he made no move to stop her.

"It's addressed to you," Skade said.

"It would be." Michael took the piece of paper out of her hand and slowly opened it. His face paled as he read.

"What does it say?"

Michael crumpled the letter in one hand and threw it on the floor. "It doesn't matter, mother. I have no choice."

"What do they want you to do?"

Michael would not meet her gaze. "Remember how I told you I wasn't guilty?"

"Yes, but..."

He took a deep breath and closed his eyes. "I lied."

Chapter 10

"Do you have him?" Terrin stared out the same window as before, but clouds covered the moon this time.

"I have him. And I brought a bit of insurance, too." The dark figure pushed a smaller figure out into the middle of the room. The smaller figure whimpered.

Terrin turned around. "And who is this?"

"Michael's brat. She was far too easy to steal." The dark figure held out the velvet bag. "What do you plan to do with Nicodemus?"

Terrin took the bag and slipped it into a pocket of his shirt. He knelt in front of the little girl and fingered her long red hair. She wore a white nightgown, now stained and torn. Her feet were bare and scratched. Tears streaked down her face.

"Tell me, child. Is your father's name Michael?"

The child nodded.

"Did you know he was a prince?" Terrin gently removed the gag from her mouth and glanced up at the dark figure who still stood beside the door. "It wasn't necessary to frighten her, Cathan."

"I think I'll be Michael for a little while longer." The shadows receded once more, and the little girl stared up at what looked to be her father's face. "I had some of the details wrong, but I don't think Skade noticed."

"You'd better hope she didn't." Terrin loosened the ropes that bound the little girl's wrists and ankles. "What's your name?"

She stared at him, then back at Cathan, who still looked like her father, "Enapay."

Cathan laughed. "Fool."

"Did you know your father was a prince?" Terrin asked again.

Enapay shook her head. A curl escaped from behind her ear and bobbed in front of her face. Terrin gently tucked it back.

"How old are you, Enapay?"

"Six."

Terrin smiled. "My Dreamer was six when I locked her in the tower. Would you like to spend the rest of your life locked in a tower?"

A fat tear rolled down Enapay's cheek. "N-no. I want my mommy!"

"Who is her mother, Cathan?"

The man who looked like Michael shrugged. "Whoever she is, she wasn't there. I peeked in on Michael, but he was alone."

"You'd do better crying for your father, child," Terrin said, and stroked her hair. "He's the only one who can save you." He picked her up and carried her over to a chair, then tied her to it. She squirmed around and tried to free herself, but the knots were tied too tightly.

"If she gets too loud, put the gag back in," Terrin said to Cathan. "I'm going to see what Nicodemus can tell us."

"You'll never guess who I saw in Michael's house," Cathan said.

"Who?"

"She thought she was hidden, but I saw her in the mirror. Mother and son are probably having a nice little reunion right now."

Terrin stiffened. "Skade was there?"

"I didn't have time to stick around," Cathan said quickly. "I wanted to bring Nicodemus back to you."

Terrin took Cathan's arm and moved away from Enapay. "How would you like to be Michael for a little while longer?"

"I'd like that," Cathan's eyes gleamed.

"Good. Let me tell you what to do."

Later, after Cathan had gone, Terrin withdrew the bloody crystal from its pouch and carried it over to a large mirror hanging on the wall. He used his spell to fashion the barriers to keep Nicodemus trapped, then crushed the crystal in his fist.

Shards of stone pierced the palm of his hand. Terrin pressed the palm of his hand to the mirror, and felt something crash against the barriers he had in place. He strengthened them without a thought.

In the iron cage, Alban screamed.

Enapay whimpered. Terrin glanced over at her. Had she heard Alban? It was impossible, really, but it would be an interesting experiment to see if the child was powerful. Terrin had no idea about her mother, but Michael had been powerful enough.

"Nicodemus, I know you're in there. You cannot refuse my summons."

A faint, shadowy form appeared in the mirror and the blood slowly faded away.

Terrin had not seen Skade's Ghost clearly when he opened the portal from Leysan, but he was long familiar with Nicodemus' mind. The Ghost in the mirror looked exactly like Nicodemus, save for the fact that he was almost uniformly gray. His eyes watched Terrin warily, expecting punishment, or worse.

"Do you know who I am?" Terrin asked.

"Yes..."

"Do you know why you're here?"

"No. Skade will kill you for this."

Terrin smiled. "She's welcome to try."

Nicodemus glared at him. Terrin experimented by tightening the bonds around him, and the Ghost's face turned white. He started to fade away.

"I don't think so." Terrin tugged on the spell and wrapped them around Nicodemus' insubstantial form. The more the Ghost struggled, the tighter the spells became. "Now. Tell me where she hid your body."

The Ghost's eyes were mad with pain. Terrin thought it very interesting that he could feel pain at all. Exactly how had Skade set up the imprisonment? Had it truly been an accident as rumors claimed?

"My...body?" Nicodemus asked.

"Yes, your body. Tell me where it is. Do you know how long you would live if we returned you to it?"

"I don't know," Nicodemus whispered. "Skade took away my memories. I only know my name."

Terrin tightened the spell around him and heard Alban's scream echo in his mind. The Ghost gasped. He sank down on his knees inside his prison and faded away.

"Damn her!" Terrin released the spell and stalked away from the mirror.

Enapay's sobs cut off in mid-cry. Terrin turned around and saw her staring at him, eyes wide and frightened. She squirmed a little on the chair.

"What are you looking at?" he snapped.

Enapay bit her lip. "I have to go to the bathroom."

Chapter 11

"Are you feeling better?" Zaira's voice echoed loudly in Teluride's ear. He opened his eyes.

"How did you know I was awake?"

Zaira shrugged. "I just did. How do you feel?"

"Better." Teluride was surprised to find that he did feel better. The nausea was gone, and the desperate pounding in his head had faded.

"I brought you some more water. Espen's busy right now, but she'll be here later on."

Zaira helped Teluride drink. The water tasted sweet on his tongue.

"What is she doing?"

"She found the vampire. The vampire found her, really. Skade will be happy."

Teluride struggled with his memories. "Skade is...the Queen of Iomar? Red hair?"

Zaira beamed. "Yes, that's her. Espen will be so happy that you've remembered."

"I'm not sure I remember the vampire," Teluride admitted. "Does he have a name?"

Zaira hesitated. "Yes. But I'm not sure he knows it yet."

Teluride remembered what she had told him before. "Oh. You know it because of your dreams."

"I know it because Skade asked me if I did, and I did." She smiled at his confusion. "If you asked me where Alban was, I'd know, but I don't know now."

"Can you ask yourself questions?" Teluride asked.

Zaira stared at him, then laughed. The laugh startled her; she stopped and put one hand over her mouth.

Teluride had no idea what her past had been like, but if she was afraid to laugh, it couldn't have been very pleasant.

"Did you know you're a very pretty little girl?" he asked, keeping his voice light.

Zaira blushed. "I'm not. My hair...my skin..."

"I asked you a question, Zaira."

Her mouth opened in a silent 'o' of surprise. She stared at him for a long moment, searching his eyes for something she did not find. Then she burst into tears and ran from the room.

Espen appeared a moment later, drying her hands on a dishtowel.

"What did you do to Zaira? She just ran past me, sobbing as if you broke her heart."

"I asked her if she knew she was pretty," Teluride said.

Espen stared at him blankly for a moment, then smiled. "Oh!" She shook her head. "You are feeling better, aren't you?"

For the first time since he awoke in Espen's care, Teluride was able to give her a smile in return.

"Much better."

"I'll go talk to Zaira. You rest."

He was only too happy to comply.

Chapter 12

Skade stared at her son in shock. "What do you mean, you lied?"

Michael tried to laugh. "I lied to you, mother. Aren't you surprised? I've done it before. And if you saw me steal Nicodemus, I must have done that as well."

Skade caught his arm before he could pull away. "I don't believe you."

He tried to shake her off, but she clung to him and pulled him around to face her. He would not meet her eyes.

"Michael, tell me the truth. I can help you!"

"Like you helped me before?" Venom laced his voice. "You did such a good job of it, mother."

Skade stared at him. "What do you mean? You wouldn't speak to me! I tried for months to get you to talk to me, but you wouldn't listen. I'd given up by the time your trial started, Michael."

"Oh, you listened," Michael spat. "You listened and you did nothing. I told you everything." He tore away from her, but did not try to flee.

"You told me nothing." Skade stood behind him, her hands outstretched. "I went to you almost every day, Michael, and you wouldn't speak to me. I didn't know what to think. We had always been so...close, and when you wouldn't speak to me..." She felt perilously close to tears.

"I don't want to talk to you anymore," Michael whispered, his head bowed. "Please leave." The white curtains billowed around him, hiding him from her sight.

Hiding him...Skade's breath caught in her throat.

"Michael, if someone wore your face when Nicodemus was taken, couldn't they have worn both yours and mine while you were in prison?"

Michael stiffened.

"And couldn't we safely assume that I was somehow diverted and never saw the real you until the end? And that you were deceived in thinking I cared nothing for your life?"

"I tried my best not to believe you were involved. I couldn't understand why you would do such a horrible thing, but the evidence against you was too great to ignore. And then when you wouldn't speak to me..."

Michael groaned. "No. It couldn't be. He wouldn't..."

"The person I saw tonight resembled you, but he resembled the younger you," Skade said. "I imagine he hadn't seen you since you were exiled."

"No. They haven't. None of them have."

"Give me names, Michael." She wanted her guess to be correct so badly.

Michael choked back a name and spun around. His face was streaked with tears. "You don't remember me telling you who set me up. You don't remember me telling you about what he did to Eabon's little girl."

"No. It wasn't me, Michael." Skade was quite sure of this now. "I swear to you it wasn't me. Do you remember me begging you to tell me the truth? Give me names, Michael, and I swear I will do everything in my power to bring them to justice."

Michael swallowed hard. "They'll kill her if I don't go along with them."

"I give you my word as the Queen of Iomar that I will not let that happen," Skade said. "I will give up my kingdom before I let my granddaughter die." Her words held a curious ring of finality that echoed faintly off the painted walls.

"You would?"

Skade nodded. "I would."

"Then I...then I suppose I should tell you their names." His voice sounded so lost. She wanted to grab hold of him and never let go, but she stayed where she was. "It was Terrin's idea. Cathan--do you remember him?-- he's the one who can mimic anyone, or anything. Nicodemus was the one who suggested they experiment on human subjects, but he Dreamed the right ingredients for their spell beforehand. And I..." he paused. "I was in charge of making sure the sickness did not spread."

"You failed," Skade said, remembering how quickly it had decimated the inhabitants of her kingdom. The sickness struck anyone with power, but subsequent healings only made it worse. The virus, or whatever they had concocted, lived on magic. Therefore, only without the use of magic did anyone survive, but Skade and Espen had not been able to find a cure. Thus the row of silent bodies in Leysan, and Nicodemus' body in Iomar. Did Terrin know they were there? She thought they were well protected, but her protections had failed twice already. Still, if he had found them, she would have known by now.

"Yes. I failed." Michael stared into the past now, his eyes unfocused. "I failed. They didn't tell me they had started to infect other people until it was too late and I couldn't stop it. The first dozen they used were willing. At least that's what Terrin told me."

"How did you stop it from spreading?" Skade asked.

"There were spells," Michael said. "I'm not sure I remember them. Here it's been twenty-eight years since I was exiled. I tried to forget as much as I could."

"You don't look twenty-eight years older," Skade said.

"I...I'm not." He hesitated. "There's not enough time to tell you right now. I have to get Enapay back."

"We have to get Enapay back," Skade said. "Would you be willing to testify against them?"

Michael met her gaze. "If I had my daughter back, I'd do just about anything to make them pay for what they did to me."

Something he had said earlier tickled the back of her mind. "What did you say about Zaira?"

"Eabon's daughter? Terrin wanted her to be stronger. He infected her with the virus, but it didn't kill her. It changed her."

"I know," Skade said, remembering her pale hair and white skin. "Why did it change her and not kill her?"

"Terrin thought it had something to do with the fact that she was a dreamer," Michael replied. "But we never found out."

"Nicodemus was infected after your arrest," Skade whispered.

"After my arrest? But I thought you had quarantined the..."

"I had. At the time, I thought he had been sick for a little while and didn't turn himself in until it was almost too late. If you had been the one responsible for it all, then you couldn't have infected him."

"Terrin's the only one who knows the full spell," Michael whispered. "I knew pieces of it, once."

"If Terrin knows the spell, then your daughter's life is in even more danger," Skade said. "You're going to have to come with me."

"I can't, remember?" Michael asked. "I can't ever go ho...back." His eyes were bright with tears again.

"I'll take care of that," Skade said. "Follow me."

She led him to the mirror, called up the portal, and turned to him. "Close your eyes."

He closed his eyes, trusting her.

For one short moment, Skade hesitated. Was this the right thing to do? She would never know the unequivocal truth; she doubted Terrin would ever confess.

But she had to start somewhere, and if Michael was innocent...

She tore the spell away before she had a chance to change her mind. Michael gasped and fell forward. Skade caught him, slung his arm over her shoulders, and helped him home.

Chapter 12

Espen found Zaira standing in front of the mirror in the bathroom with tears running down her face. She leaned in the doorway and watched her for a moment, then cleared her throat.

"I heard Teluride asked you a question you couldn't answer."

Zaira sniffed and turned away from the mirror. "I'm not pretty."

"Well, honey, I guess it depends on who you ask. Teluride seems to think you are." She kept her voice purposefully light. "Why don't we ask someone else for their opinion?"

"I'm not pretty," Zaira said again. Her voice dropped to a whisper. "Skade is pretty."

"Skade is very pretty," Espen agreed. "But that doesn't mean you're not. You can't look like Skade, just like Skade can't look like you."

"No one would want to look like me." Zaira turned away from the mirror.

Espen stepped behind her and turned her back to face it. "Look at yourself, child." She saw Zaira take a tiny peek at herself. "No, honey, really look at yourself." Espen lifted one of Zaira's hands and placed it against the child's cheek. The bruises had faded, leaving unmarked skin behind.

"When I was a little girl, I wanted to have skin as pale as yours," Espen said.

Zaira stared up at her. "Really? Why?"

"Because people with skin like mine weren't treated very nicely. And people with skin like yours were."

"I think you're pretty," Zaira whispered.

Espen laughed. "Thank you. Do you want to know a secret?"

"I know a lot of secrets," Zaira said. "But yes. Tell me."

"This is one you don't know yet."

"Tell me!"

"Do you know you're a very pretty little girl?"

The vampire awoke from a dream that left him drained and aching. He opened his eyes, expecting to see the seeping walls of his cell, but he saw white painted walls instead.

He turned his head and realized he lay in someone's bed. Whose bed? Had he been rescued? Were the bed and the white walls part of a dream?

He remembered a long row of beds, but nothing else. A mirror, perhaps, and rats... Slowly, his memory returned. Espen. The mirror.

Freedom.

He raised his head; saw a shuttered window above a small table that held a vase of purple flowers. He raised one arm, and saw that someone had cleaned the filth from his skin. He wore an oversized white shirt and little else.

The room would have been dim to normal sight, but he felt comfortable in soothing darkness without any rats to bother him. He lay back down and fell asleep while waiting for someone to open the door.

When he awoke, a pale little girl stood beside his bed, quietly waiting for him to open his eyes. The vampire recognized her at once.

"You're Zaira, aren't you?"

She nodded and bit her lip. "I'm sorry if I woke you."

He felt at ease around this child as he had not felt at ease around anyone else. Perhaps it was her small stature. Perhaps it was because he had known her the longest, although he doubted she remembered him.

"You didn't wake me up." He started to sit up and she helped plump the pillows under his back.

"I have a question to ask you," Zaira said when he was comfortable again. "Two questions, really."

"What kind of questions?" the vampire asked.

"Do you know your name yet? Espen said I could tell you if you didn't know."

"I know my name." It still didn't feel like his name. He didn't think it ever would.

Zaira beamed. "Good!"

The vampire gave her a hesitant smile. "What's your second question?"

She hesitated. "It's really a silly question. I probably shouldn't ask you."

"I don't think there are any silly questions."

"Do you think I'm pretty?" Zaira blurted, and dropped her gaze, as if afraid of his reply.

The question threw him off guard, but he caught himself before he said anything that could be taken the wrong way. He studied her for a moment.

"Yes, I do."

She stared at him. "You really do?"

"I really do."

Zaira slowly leaned over and kissed him on the cheek. "Thank you. I'll go tell Espen you're awake."

Chapter 14

After much deliberation centering on the fact that Terrin did not want to have to take the little girl to the bathroom every five minutes, he had tied a long rope to her ankle and tethered it to a heavy table on the other side of the room.

She had stopped crying as soon as they locked the door behind them. Nicodemus watched her silently, until she glanced his way.

"Are you really a ghost?"

Pain from Terrin's spell made it hard to concentrate on questions.

"Yes, I'm really a ghost. My name is Nicodemus."

The little girl cocked her head. "My name is Enapay. I'm six."

Nicodemus couldn't remember ever being six. He watched as she got to her feet and tried to make the rope reach the mirror, but her fingers barely touched the frame.

"I can't reach you, Nic-o-de-mus." She had to sound out his name. "Is my daddy going to find me here?"

Nicodemus hoped she wouldn't start crying again. "I hope so."

"If my daddy finds me here, he'll find you too, won't he?"

Nicodemus nodded. "I hope so." He wondered if he could contact Skade, or if Terrin's spells would prevent him from using this mirror like he used hers. He had to try; it might be their only hope. But could he push away the pain long enough to send her a message?

He reached out to touch the spells that bound him and hissed as a bolt of pain traveled up his arm. He pushed through it anyway, determined to reach his Queen.

"Nic-o-demus?" Enapay stared at him.

"It hurts," he whispered, and fell back against the mirror. "I don't think I can reach her, Enapay."

"Reach who?" Enapay asked.

The jolt of power made his hand twitch despite his efforts to keep it still. "Skade. Your grandmother. Can you...can you untie the rope?"

"I have a grandmother?"

He pushed harder, but the stubborn spell would not let him go. He whimpered.

Enapay worked at the rope, picking at it with less-than-coordinated fingers. "I can't get it."

"Try harder," Nicodemus gasped. The pain tore at his defenses, demanding release, but he didn't want to scream.

His arm began to burn. Faint wisps of gray drifted up from where the spell met ghostly flesh and he watched as his skin began to blister and peel. He pushed harder, but the spell still would not give way.

"I did it!" Enapay beamed and held up the rope.

"Come here," Nicodemus whispered. "Touch the mirror."

Enapay hesitated, then placed one hand flat on the mirror. The spells rippled. Nicodemus groaned.

"It's hurting you," Enapay whispered.

"Terrin will hurt you worse." Nicodemus placed his other hand against the mirror. "I'm going to send you somewhere safe, Enapay. I want you to tell Skade that I'm in Leysan. Can you remember that?"

"Leysan," Enapay murmured. "I'll remember."

"Okay." Pain almost robbed him of speech. "When I tell you to step through the mirror, step through. Don't hesitate. Do you understand?"

Enapay nodded solemnly.

"If you remember, tell Skade that Alban is in an iron cage in the dungeons. He's a vampire. Tell her I couldn't find the vampire anywhere, but I found one of her beads in the dungeons. He might have escaped."

"A vampire," Enapay whispered. "Beads. He might have escaped."

Nicodemus glanced down at his arm and saw gray bone where no bone should be. He wondered if he could heal as a ghost. He had healed before, hadn't he? Or would he lose his arm to save a little girl's life?

Either way, he could not let Terrin have her. He thrust his arm further in the mass of spells and felt something break.

Quickly, before Terrin could realize what he had done, he formed a sloppy portal to Iomar and fed it through the break in the spell.

"Now, Enapay. Step through the mirror." He held the portal open by will alone. He could no longer see her face, but he felt the spells shudder over his body when she stepped into the portal.

The mirror in Iomar shattered. Nicodemus opened his eyes as the portal collapsed on top of him. The backlash of magic drove him back against Terrin's spells.

This time, he could not help but scream.

Chapter 15

Michael slipped out of Skade's grip and fell away, into the portal. She grabbed for him, missed, and the portal skewed sideways, throwing her out of the mirror.

She turned back for her son and saw a roiling mass of dark clouds behind the glass, obscuring her sight.

"Michael!"

The clouds boiled. Her son did not appear.

Skade placed one hand on the mirror and concentrated her will, driving the clouds back. She felt something snap and reverberate against the glass. For a moment, she thought the mirror might shatter, but it held. Barely.

Quickly, before she lost her grip, Skade reached into the clouds. Her hand brushed skin and she grabbed a handful of his shirt and pulled him backwards.

He collapsed beside her, breathing heavily, his eyes glazed with pain.

Skade helped Michael up and lowered him to her bed.

Just as she turned back to close the portal, the mirror exploded, showering the entire room with shards of glass.

Skade stood frozen in the middle of the room. From behind her, she heard Michael clear his throat.

"Did I do that?"

"No." She didn't think it had been some remnant of the spell. "I don't think so, at least. My maids are going to be furious. They just finished cleaning up all the blood."

"Blood?" Michael brushed glass off his pajamas and picked a piece of shrapnel out of the palm of his hand.

"Your double killed one of my maids to free Nicodemus from that mirror," Skade said. "I wonder if he was trying to get back." She picked up one of the largest pieces of glass and stared into it. After a moment, she handed the piece of glass to Michael.

It only took him a second to see what she had seen in the shard. "Enapay." He stared up at her. "Is she..."

"In there? No. I don't think so, but it wouldn't hurt to check."

"How can you check?"

"I might be able to reconstruct it if there aren't any pieces missing." Skade stared at the empty frame.

"Reconstruct it? How?"

"Just watch." Skade extended her hands towards the empty frame. She sent out a wave of power, not a tendril, and swept the room for glass. She heard Michael gasp behind her, but ignored him in favor of putting the mirror back together.

The shreds of the portal still hung in the air beyond the mirror, and she patched it back together as she pieced together the mirror itself.

"Enapay!"

"Daddy?"

The pieces of the portal grew too unwieldy to hold. Skade tried to follow it back to its source, but she lost it halfway there. This time, when the mirror shattered, it collapsed into sparkling dust.

Nicodemus had created it, though. His pain had colored every piece of it. Skade hoped he was still alive.

A small hand tugged on her dress. "Are you Skade?"

Skade glanced down at her granddaughter. "How did you know my name?"

"Nic-o-demus told me."

"Nicodemus made that portal for you, didn't he?" Skade knelt in front of the little girl and ignored her son hovering behind his daughter.

The child nodded. "It hurt him, though."

Remembering the spells he had pulled away from Teluride, Skade could imagine creating the portal had hurt him quite badly.

"Do you know where you were, Enapay?" Skade asked. Did Terrin know Nicodemus could die? Did she want him to know?

"Nic-o-demus said Leysan," Enapay said carefully. "He said to tell you Alban is a vampire in an iron cage."

"Alban is a vampire? Or Alban is with the vampire?" Surely Terrin hadn't done the unthinkable.

Enapay shook her head. "Alban is in an iron cage and he's a vampire."

Skade closed her eyes and bowed her head. "Michael, Terrin has Leysan blocked against me. There isn't anything I can do to rescue Alban or the vampire."

"The vampire!" Enapay tugged on her dress again. "Nic-o-demus said..." she frowned, "He found a bead. But not the vampire."

Skade remembered the bracelet she had given Alban. Nicodemus had been able to see through it once; it only made sense that he would look for that link again.

"Thank you, Enapay."

The little girl beamed. "You're welcome."

Skade stared at her son and her granddaughter and felt tears gather in her eyes. She sat down on her bed and stared at the empty frame.

"Michael, I can't get into Leysan. Terrin has it blocked against my magic."

"What does that have to do with me?" Michael asked.

Skade patted the bed and Enapay climbed up to sit beside her. "You have a very smart little girl."

"And you're avoiding my question," Michael said.

"No, I'm not. I'm just trying to think it through before I propose it to you." She bit her lip. "Terrin doesn't know you're here with me. I doubt Nicodemus will tell him where he sent Enapay, unless he's too hurt to resist. Even if Terrin knows she's here, he doesn't know about you. As far as he is concerned, you're on your way to do whatever they told you to do."

"To save my daughter's life," Michael whispered, understanding dawning in his eyes.

"Exactly."

"You want me to go to Leysan."

"Yes."

"And pretend I don't know Enapay is safe."

Out loud, her plan sounded very shaky, but it was the only one Skade had been able to come up with.

"Yes."

Michael closed his eyes. "You want me to play the traitor; to play right into their hands?"

"There's a catch," Skade whispered.

"There always is."

Thirty minutes later, Skade carried the mirror from the bathroom into her bedroom and propped it against the empty frame. It only took her a moment to call up the connection to Espen's cottage deep in the woods.

She glanced back at Enapay to make sure the little girl hadn't moved from her place on the other side of the room where she could not been seen in the mirror.

Michael stood nearby, also unseen.

"It took you long enough," Espen said as soon as she turned around. "What's going on? I tried to reach your usual mirror, but I couldn't get through."

"Espen, I have something very important to tell you," Skade said, dispensing with formalities. She had no time for small talk. Not if she wanted to make this work.

"As do I." The older witch raised one ebony eyebrow. "I think it might be a good idea if I go first."

Skade folded her arms. "If you insist."

"The vampire is here with me," Espen said. "He escaped from his cell using your bracelet, somehow, and he ended up in the same room as the sleepers. When he tried to use the mirror to contact you, I brought him here."

"How did he get into that room?" Skade gasped.

"I blocked his entrance already. I'm not sure how we missed it the first time, but it was a tiny hole."

"Did he..." Skade could just imagine what would have happened if the vampire tried to drink infected blood.

"No." The same thought had already occurred to Espen. "Terrin hurt him badly, but he used your beads to survive."

"He used my beads?"

Espen shrugged. "He told me they turned into blood. He also told me..."

"That Alban is a vampire?" Skade guessed.

"How did you know?"

"Terrin's been busy. He stole Nicodemus right out from under my nose, and he kidnapped my granddaughter. We have her back, now, but Terrin still has Nicodemus."

Espen's eyes narrowed. "Your granddaughter? We?"

Skade ignored her. "Someone named Cathan put on Michael's face and murdered one of my maids to get Nicodemus. I thought Michael had broken the spell and returned here, so I asked my mirror to find him."

"And you found him?"

"I found him, but someone kidnapped his daughter while I was there. Espen, he's innocent!" She still could not believe how stupid she had been.

"Skade, where is Michael now?" Espen leaned forward, searching the background, but Michael was not yet in sight.

"I broke the spell and brought him here with me. He's right here..." Michael moved on the edge of her vision, and Skade glanced over at him. He smiled at her.

Something in his smile didn't quite add up. She started to turn around.

Something heavy smashed into the back of her head. Skade pitched forward, catching herself on the edge of the empty frame. She heard Espen shout just before the connection terminated, and managed to get one arm up to protect her head as Michael hit her again.

Her own son. Sadness lodged in her chest and prevented her from calling for the guards. She had not just been tricked. She had fallen for it hook, line, and sinker. She had wanted to believe him innocent, and so he had portrayed himself. And she had believed him.

She saw Michael bending over her, saw his hand come away from the back of her head red with blood. She felt him lift her, saw his lips form words she could not hear.

For the first time in her life, Skade felt herself drift downward into darkness, and she did not fight the descent.

Chapter 16

"You're not my daddy!"

Terrin heard Enapay's voice long before Cathan appeared in the doorway with his prisoners, still wearing Michael's guise.

"Gag her or kill her; I don't care which," Cathan growled. "If I have to hear her whining little voice again, I'll kill her myself." He noticed the blood seeping out of the mirror. "What happened?"

"Nicodemus opened the portal that collided with Skade's," Terrin said. "Now we know what happens when two different people try to use the same mirror at the same time."

"Is he dead?"

"No." Terrin turned away from the mirror. "But he will soon wish he was."

He opened a small door at the other end of the room and Cathan lowered his burden to the narrow bed inside. The Queen of Iomar had yet to awaken, but Terrin knew they had to take steps if they wished to hold her for any period of time.

He held out a pair of silver scissors and a large velvet bag. "I want every bead she is wearing put inside this bag before she wakes up."

Cathan nodded. His face started to shimmer, but Terrin stopped him.

"Stay Michael until I tell you otherwise," he said. "We want her to think he betrayed her."

"She figured out I had become him to steal Nicodemus," Cathan said. "She'll figure this out soon enough."

"Not if we keep her guessing," Terrin said. "Don't worry. I do have a plan."

"Where did you put him?" Cathan asked.

Terrin smiled. "Somewhere safe. I have no doubt he'll cooperate with us once he realizes I will not hesitate to kill the child."

A dull knocking sound reached their ears. Terrin turned to see Enapay rap on the mirror again.

"Nic-o-demus?"

When she saw him watching, she backed up into the corner and scrunched up into a little ball.

"You're not my daddy."

Cathan laughed softly. "You're right; I'm not. Your daddy wouldn't kill you. I would."

Enapay's eyes filled with tears.

Terrin walked over to her and crouched down in front of her. "Enapay, would you like to see your daddy?"

The little girl nodded.

"If you want to see your daddy again, then you must be a very good little girl. Do you think you can do that?"

She nodded again.

Terrin grabbed her hand and pulled her up. She tried to fight him, but he was much too strong for her. He dragged her over to the mirror.

Cathan watched from the doorway of Skade's cell.

"The beads, Cathan. Before she wakes up."

"What are you going to do?" Cathan asked, mesmerized by Enapay's tears.

"Put her somewhere where she won't bother us again," Terrin said. "I need someone to find Nicodemus anyway."

"I thought you said he wasn't dead."

"He's not. I know he's not dead, but I still can't find him. There's too much...debris."

Enapay hiccupped a sob. "I'll be a good girl," she whispered.

Terrin smiled. "I'm sure you will be." He took a small dagger from his belt, and drew the blade across the palm of Enapay's little hand. "This might hurt."

She screamed.

Cathan clapped his hands over his ears and scowled. "She's going to wake her up."

"Then you'd better have taken away her source of power," Terrin growled. He jerked Enapay towards the mirror and smeared her blood over the glass.

The mirror shimmered, casting strange shadows over the room. Enapay's blood began to sizzle on the glass, and a horrible smell poured out of the mirror. It smelled like...Terrin stepped back. Like burning flesh.

For a short moment, he hesitated. He didn't want to kill the girl, after all, just put her out of reach for a little while.

When the smell faded, he made up his mind and smiled down at Enapay. "You're going to be a good little girl and find Nicodemus for me, aren't you?"

Enapay stared up at him with tears pouring down her face. "Y...yes."

"When you find him, I'll let you go."

"Terrin, can she live in there?" Cathan asked, aghast despite his previous words.

Terrin lifted Enapay and lowered her into the mirror. She vanished from his sight. "We'll know soon enough. Do you have the beads?"

Cathan held up the velvet bag.

"Good. Now we can get to work."

Chapter 17

Pain. His whole world was pain. Each pulse of the spell sent a new wave of agony crashing over him, leaving little room for coherent thought.

Something touched his arm. What felt like a small hand closed over his wrist and pulled him away from the spell.

Even when released, his body still on fire from the pain, he could do nothing but lie on the floor of his cell and wait to die.

"Nic-o-demus?"

"Enapay?" His heart sank. He had sacrificed everything, only to fail.

"I saw my daddy, but he wasn't my daddy anymore," Enapay said. "You're smoking."

"I...I think I might be dying," Nicodemus whispered. He cracked open his eyes and saw her sitting with her back against the mirror, solid and completely whole.

His mind didn't want to think about why this was so extraordinary, but he couldn't stop the agonizing process of thought.

"You're...here."

"I didn't think ghosts could die," Enapay said. "I thought Ghosts are already dead."

Memories stirred in Nicodemus' mind. "I'm...not dead." More memories erupted, freed by the force of Terrin's spell and the backlash that had nearly killed him. "I'm not dead."

"Then you're not a ghost."

Nicodemus noticed that she held one hand close to her chest, and that her white nightgown was spotted with blood.

"What did he do to you?"

"He cut my hand," Enapay whispered. "It hurts."

That seemed to be important, but Nicodemus had no idea why. He pushed it away for later.

"I thought I felt you go through the portal," he whispered, trying to remember what had happened through the pain. "I thought I felt Skade..."

"Skade's here."

"Here? What do you mean?"

"The man who isn't my daddy hurt her and brought her here."

"Your daddy's name is Michael, isn't it?" He remembered Michael. He remembered what he had Dreamed, and cursed himself for being such a fool.

Skade's spell had been broken. His memories were back. Did that mean he would also be able to Dream again?

"Ask me a question, Enapay." He pushed away the pain and tried to focus on her face. "Ask me a question."

"Where is my daddy?"

Nicodemus saw Michael's bloody face rise up in his mind. "He's in a room not far from this one. Four doors down. He's unconscious. Ask me another question."

"Who's the black lady in Skade's mirror?" Enapay asked, smiling a little at his enthusiasm.

"Her name is Espen. She's a witch." Nicodemus remembered her from before and wondered if he'd ever get a chance to apologize.

He took a deep breath. "Enapay, I want you to ask me one more question, but I'm going to tell you what it is, okay?"

Sensing the game wasn't a game anymore, she nodded solemnly.

"Ask me..." Hundreds of questions ran through his mind. He hardly felt the pain now; it had been buried under newfound hope. "Ask me...what does Terrin plan to do?"

Enapay repeated the question.

Nicodemus closed his eyes. When the first vision came, he was unprepared for the violence of it. It speared his mind and left him cringing away from the future Terrin envisioned.

"What does Terrin plan to do?" Enapay asked again.

Nicodemus cracked open his eyes. "Destroy the world," he whispered. "Ask me...ask me how to stop him."

"How do you stop..."

The mirror shimmered behind her. Terrin reached through, grabbed a handful of hair, and pulled her out of Nicodemus' prison.

"The next time you want to deceive me into thinking you're dead, try not to project what you see through the mirror." Terrin smiled. "But you can project all you want when I ask you the questions."

Nicodemus let his head fall back. So close. He'd been so close.

He heard Enapay scream something on the other side of the mirror, but he couldn't make out her words.

"You've regained your memories, haven't you?"

"Yes." They stirred in his mind uneasily.

"Good. Where did Skade hide your body?"

He did not have the ease of long practice to only answer with half-truths.

"In Iomar. In the dungeons."

"How do I get past her spells?"

Nicodemus had no choice but to tell him.

Chapter 18

Skade struggled out of darkness to find she lay on a narrow bed in an unfamiliar room. What had happened? The last thing she remembered...

"Oh, Michael." She raised one hand to the back of her throbbing head and felt sticky blood matted in her hair. In the years since she had been crowned, no one had ever dared to strike her. Her own son. Why had he betrayed her?

"I see you're awake." Terrin stood in the doorway, arms crossed. "How do you feel?"

Skade winced as his voice bounced inside her skull. "Like I've been hit with a hammer." She saw no reason to lie.

"I think he said he used a vase," Terrin said. "But what he used doesn't really matter, does it?"

Skade struggled to sit up. She would not lie helpless, even though her head felt like it would split open from the pressure.

"What did you promise him?" she asked. "Why did he betray me?"

"I promised him nothing. Perhaps your son merely wanted to be with his friends."

"You set him up!" Skade struggled to keep hold of her temper. "You destroyed his life!"

"He seems to have made a nice one to replace the one he lost." Terrin stepped inside the room and closed the door behind him. "I've always wondered if you were as powerful as you seem to claim." He held up a black velvet bag. "Do you want to guess what's inside this bag?"

Skade had already realized her beads were gone. Her hand rose to her bare throat, then dropped to her lap.

"Do you think I'm stupid enough to keep all my power in my jewelry?"

Terrin did not smile. "I can feel the magic in your beads without even trying."

Skade shrugged. "That's only power-by-contact. I wear them all the time. It's only fitting that they would hold some of my power."

"So if I destroy them, you won't feel a thing?"

Damn him. Was she that obvious? She could sever all ties to the beads, but that would take a long time, and she might miss one or two. And if he planned to destroy them all at once, she didn't have a chance.

"Answer my question."

"And if I do not?"

Terrin shrugged. "Then I ask Nicodemus. He has his memory back, by the way. Your spell didn't survive for long."

First the pain of the portal backlash, and then the pain of his memories. Skade marveled that Nicodemus was still sane.

"Then ask him," she whispered. At least that would buy her some time.

"Michael, watch your mother and make sure she doesn't try any spells," Terrin said, and turned away from the door. "I have another question to ask our dreamer."

Michael appeared in the doorway, his face shuttered and still. Skade turned away from him, disgusted with herself for believing his lies.

"I only wanted you to break the spell, Mother," he whispered. "I wanted to break the spell so I could come back. And you did everything I asked."

"You are no son of mine." Skade clenched her teeth against the urge to hurt him and concentrated on the beads. She could handle forgetting one or two, but not the whole bunch. If Terrin destroyed them all at once, the backlash was likely to kill her.

"Where's Enapay, Michael? What happened to rescuing her? I gave you my word I would not stand to see her harmed."

"Your word is worth nothing if you're dead," Michael snapped. "My daughter is..."

He vanished from the doorway. Skade stood and followed him in time to see him lunge and catch Enapay just before she reached a large mirror hanging on the wall.

"Give her to me." Skade held out her arms. "At least let me spend a little time with my granddaughter before I die."

Michael hesitated.

"Give me that much. Please." She continued to sever the beads' power as she spoke and felt it start to trickle out of the bag.

"Give her the girl," Terrin snapped. "Since you can't seem to tie a proper knot, we might as well have all our prisoners in one place."

Michael shoved Enapay towards the door. She tried to run, but he grabbed the back of her nightgown and hauled her inside. Then he slammed the door and locked it.

Enapay stood and dusted herself off. "That's not my daddy," she said, and burst into tears.

Chapter 19

Zaira heard something crash in the kitchen. She ran into the room to find Espen attempting to put out a fire that threatened to consume the kitchen table.

"What happened?"

Espen lowered the charred dishcloth and stared at the melted remains of a small mirror. "I wish I knew. I was in the middle of a conversation with Skade, and all hell broke loose."

Zaira bit her lip. "I could tell you."

"I know you could, honey. And I might have to ask you, if I can't get Skade back." She sighed. "Will you bring me another mirror? There should be one in the hall."

When Zaira returned with another mirror, Espen had cleaned off the table, leaving only a scorch mark behind. Zaira watched as Espen set the second mirror up and tried to connect to Iomar.

After fifteen minutes of trying, she gave up.

"I'm really sorry to do this to you, Zaira. I know I promised you I wouldn't, but I'm worried about Skade."

"I understand." Espen still looked troubled. Zaira smiled. "Really. I don't mind. Not for you."

"Where's Skade?" Espen asked. "What happened in Iomar?"

The visions bloomed in Zaira's mind. She waited a moment to make sure she had all of it, then frowned.

"Skade isn't in Iomar anymore."

Espen laughed. "I gathered that."

"She's a prisoner in Leysan. With a little girl." Zaira glanced at Espen's face.

"Her granddaughter, I presume."

"Her name is Enapay. She's six."

Espen nodded. "Where is Skade's son, Zaira?"

"He's in Leysan too." Zaira closed her eyes and shook her head. "It doesn't make sense."

"What doesn't make sense?"

"I see two people. One of them is tied up not far away from Skade and Enapay. The other one is with Terrin. But they both look the same." She opened her eyes. "I don't understand."

"Before we were disconnected, Skade told me she had figured out that someone named Cathan had 'put on Michael's face'. Which one of them is Cathan?"

Zaira did not hesitate. "The one with Terrin."

"How long has Michael been tied up?"

"Since Skade brought him through the portal. She lost him for a little while, and that's when he was captured."

"And that's when Cathan came through, I bet." Espen's mouth set in a thin line. "I bet Skade thinks Michael betrayed her."

"She does. But Enapay knows the other Michael isn't the right one."

"Thank you, Zaira. You've helped me a great deal."

"I can tell you more," Zaira offered.

Espen smiled at her. "I know you can. But I am of the mind that you don't want to know too much of the future, because it might come true."

Zaira frowned. "But isn't it supposed to come true?"

"Why don't you go keep Alexander company?" Espen asked, not answering her question. "I think he's awake. I have some thinking to do."

"Are you going to rescue Skade?" Zaira asked. "And Michael? And Enapay?"

"And Nicodemus," Espen said. "We can't forget about him."

"He's..." Zaira had never volunteered information before. "He has his memory back."

"Does he?" Espen busied herself at the sink, dumping out old tea and putting the kettle back on to boil.

"So Terrin knows everything you know," Zaira said. "It would be best if you asked me what they're going to do next."

Espen grew very still. "What are they going to do next?"

Zaira told her.

Chapter 20

"What do you mean, he's not your daddy?" Skade asked.

Enapay wiped her eyes. "He's not my daddy. My daddy isn't mean. My daddy is nice, like Nic-o-demus."

"Your daddy hit me on the head and brought me here," Skade said, wondering if his declaration of innocence had been a lie. Had he used her so easily?

Enapay shook her head. "That wasn't my daddy. My daddy's in a room. Four doors down. Un-conscious." She sounded as if she repeated this from rote.

"Who told you that?" Skade asked.

"Nic-o-demus. He wanted me to ask him a question, so I did."

If that was Cathan outside the door, then had she ever spoken to the real Michael? Had it all been a farce? She had broken the spell that prevented him from returning to Iomar. Surely that had been her son. But when had Terrin taken him?

And then she remembered. The portal. Having to repair it to find him, and how dazed he had been when she pulled him out. How he had not hugged his daughter when she escaped through Nicodemus' portal. How he had so easily agreed to go to Leysan.

"Where did you say he was?" she asked.

"Four doors down. Un-conscious."

"What else did Nicodemus tell you?" Skade asked. It made sense that his talent would return with his memories. She hadn't thought of that.

"He told me to ask him another question," Enapay said.

"What did you ask him?"

"Who the black lady was in your mirror. Nic-o-demus said her name was Espen and she's a witch."

"She is." Skade wished her head would stop pounding so she could concentrate on what she had to do. She couldn't concentrate on Enapay, her head, and the beads at the same time. Something had to go, and the headache would be her first choice.

"And then he told me to ask him what Terrin planned to do, but he didn't tell me what it was." Enapay wiped her nose on her sleeve and yawned.

Skade realized her granddaughter was only six, after all. "Would you like to lie down? I'll watch over you for as long as I can." She thought she must be halfway through the bag of beads by now, and wondered why Terrin hadn't noticed the magic leaking out of his bag.

"An' then..." Enapay curled up on the bed and stared at Skade. "An' then he told me to ask him how to stop Terrin, but I wasn't fast enough."

"That was a smart thing to ask him," Skade said. "Was it your idea or his?"

Enapay closed her eyes. "His."

"Did you hear what Terrin asked him?" Skade had a good idea what his first question would have been.

"'bout his body," Enapay murmured.

Skade remembered what Michael, the real Michael, had said.

"Eabon's daughter? Terrin wanted her to be stronger. He infected her with the virus, but it didn't kill her. It changed her."

Would Nicodemus die if Terrin forced him back into his body, or would he end up changed, like Zaira? What would he do, after ten years as a ghost?

Skade would rather not find out, but she knew she didn't have much of a choice in her current position. She needed help, but her only hope was a six-year-old child.

The future, with or without dreams, did not look good.

Chapter 21

Before he lost his memory and became the Ghost in Skade's mirror, Nicodemus had used his talent for many horrible things. He had enjoyed making other people miserable at his own expense. He had used his dreams for profit, and little else.

Now, with ten years of amnesia behind him, he realized Skade had been correct. He had changed. And now he wanted no part of the person he had been before.

He watched as the fake Michael tormented Skade, and wished he could tell her the truth. But Terrin's questions had left him drained and weak, and the spell still sapped his energy.

Nicodemus no longer thought he was dying, but he had come very close to oblivion. Even now, he wondered if that would have been best. Dead, he would not have been able to help Terrin. Dead, he would be free of both pain and the memories, and he wouldn't have to worry about what would happen next.

He did not stir when Terrin and Cathan left. He lay in his cell and watched the magic that had escaped Skade's beads, staining the air outside the mirror in various shades of the rainbow. Even though Terrin had taken the bag with him, the magic remained. He heard nothing from Skade or Enapay until he realized the faint whisper drifting through the mirror came from Skade.

Nicodemus raised his head. "My Queen?" Old habits died hard. It took nearly all of his strength to stand.

"I think it's safe for you to call me by name, Nicodemus." He could not see her, but he could imagine the look on her face. "I have a question to ask you."

Nicodemus shivered. "Ask."

"Two questions, and I apologize," Skade said. "The first one: How can I get out of here? The second one: How do we stop Terrin?"

Nicodemus fell to his knees, too weak to stand. "The answer to the first question: Use the magic released from your beads. Can you see it?"

"It's a little hard to see through a solid door, Nicodemus."

"It's drifting around out here," Nicodemus whispered. "Draw it back into yourself. It's your magic, after all. It hasn't changed."

Skade was silent for a moment. "That might work," she finally said. "Thank you."

"The answer to your second question..." Nicodemus gasped.

"What is it?" Skade asked.

"Nothing." He said it too quickly; she would realize he held something back. "I see three possibilities."

"I have a feeling you see more than three possibilities," Skade said.

"You're right. I do." Nicodemus took a deep breath. "There's nothing you can do about it, Skade. Even if you try, you'll fail."

"There's nothing I can do about what?"

He had to force himself not to flinch away from the tone of her voice. He didn't want to say it out loud, for fear that it would come true, but three out of four possibilities stacked the odds against him.

"I'm going to die," Nicodemus whispered. "I'm...I'm sorry, my Queen. I can't find a way around it." His voice shook. "Do you know where Terrin and Cathan went?"

"To fetch your body, I presume?"

"I don't want to die," he whispered. "I don't want to die."

"Nicodemus, listen to me." Skade's voice shook him out of misery. Ten years of conditioning forced him to pay attention.

"I'm listening."

"I don't want you to die either," Skade said. "Did you know Terrin infected Zaira with the virus and she didn't die?"

"No. I didn't know that. But what does that have to do with me?"

"I'm going to ask you another question, Nicodemus. I want you to tell me the truth."

"I never lie."

"I know." Her voice softened. "If Terrin forces you back into your body, will you die? Or will you be changed, like Zaira?"

Fear locked his voice in his throat, but he had to answer her. "It will...it will change me, like Zaira." He already knew he would not die from that.

"Nicodemus, why won't you die when everyone else did? What makes you so special?"

"The Dreams," Nicodemus whispered. "The Dreams."

"How can I cure the sleepers?"

The answer was so obvious, but it made no sense at all. He frowned.

"How can I cure the sleepers?" Skade asked again.

"By giving them a dream from the dreamer who doesn't dream," Nicodemus whispered. "But I don't understand."

Chapter 22

"I don't like knowing the future," Zaira whispered to the vampire.

He opened his eyes. "I didn't like it either. What happened?"

"A lot." Zaira told him everything she had told Espen. "You used to Dream?"

"A long time ago," the vampire whispered. "Terrin took that away when he stole my name." After telling Skade what he had done, the specter of it wasn't so horrible anymore. "The dreaming didn't come back with my name."

"No one's asked you any questions yet," Zaira said.

Trust Zaira to realize that. The vampire sighed. "No, they haven't."

"Do you want me to try?"

He never wanted to dream again, but if a simple test made her forget what she had seen for a little while, the vampire thought he could survive.

"Ask me a question."

Zaira glanced back at the door. "Teluride wants to ask me a question, but he isn't sure he wants to know the answer. Do you think if I ask you..."

"It won't hurt to try," the vampire said. "What's the question?"

"Will Teluride ever get his memory back?"

Nothing stirred in his mind. No answer, no vision, no dream. The vampire sighed. "It didn't work."

"Maybe I didn't ask the right question," Zaira said. "Do you want to try again?"

He had grown so used to the absence of both name and power. He had his name back; whatever good that would do for him, but the power remained stubbornly absent.

But hadn't he felt something when he opened the portal in the mirror?

"I don't think so," he whispered. "But I would like to do a little experiment." He sat up straighter and curled his legs under him. "Do you think you can find me a small mirror?"

"Espen melted hers, but I bet I can find one somewhere," Zaira said. "Can I help with your experiment?"

"Sure." The vampire doubted it would work, but he had to try.

When Zaira returned with a mirror no larger than the palm of her hand, he held it up in front of his face and stared into it. Without the filth and with regular feedings, he could almost pass for human.

"What are you going to do?" Zaira asked.

"When I escaped from the dungeons, I used a mirror to contact Skade," the vampire explained. "I didn't really understand what I was doing at the time, but I think I understand now."

He bit his thumb until it bled, and then spread the blood across the mirror's face. "I want to see my brother."

The mirror shimmered and the blood slowly faded away. The vampire used the edge of a sheet for a bandage, twisting it around his finger without much care for staining Espen's sheets.

The mirror turned black. After a minute or two, it lightened enough for him to see a small room and an iron cage. And inside the iron cage...

His hand shook when he showed the scene to Zaira. She seemed duly impressed.

"Can you find anyone else?" She climbed up beside him and stared at the mirror. "What about Nicodemus? What about Skade?"

"Show me Nicodemus," the vampire whispered, and the mirror changed. This time, it showed the inside of another mirror, and Nicodemus, Skade's Ghost, who lay curled up on the floor of his prison.

"I think we need to show this to Espen," Zaira said. "She can't get the mirror to do this."

"I think that would be a good idea," the vampire agreed. "And I think I know why I can find them when no one else can."

"Why?"

"Because my father used what was left of my powers to create the spell," the vampire said. "If I'm right, I should be able to break it so Espen can go in."

"And if you're wrong?"

He didn't want to think about what would happen if he was wrong. "You're going to tell me if I'm right or wrong, but only after we tell Espen. Is that okay?"

Zaira nodded.

"Good." He swung his legs over the side of the bed and slowly stood with Zaira's help. "Let's go tell her and see what she says."

"She'll think it's a great idea," Zaira assured him, but he hadn't asked her a question, so he had no idea if she was right or wrong.

Chapter 23

By the time Terrin and Cathan returned with his body, Nicodemus had regained his composure enough to realize he would be in a very precarious position once Terrin completed the spell to return to his body. Skade had told him he could die as a ghost, but it was much easier to die while alive.

He stared at the bundle between them, unable to tear his eyes away. What would it feel like to be alive again? And what would Skade do if everyone survived at the end? He did not look forward to what would happen next.

The spells shimmered around him, and Nicodemus felt a presence behind him. He turned around, but the presence was gone as quickly as it had come, sinking back into nothingness.

"What was that?" Terrin asked. "Haven't you learned your lesson?"

"It wasn't me." The pain still ate away at his defenses. He doubted he could take much more of it without losing his mind.

"Your instructions for getting past Skade's spells were perfect," Terrin said. "Now I need to know how to put you back in your proper place."

"What if...what if I don't want to go?"

"I didn't give you a choice, Nicodemus." Terrin waited until Cathan dragged a long table into the room, then helped him lift the body onto it. Then they stripped the coverings and laid Nicodemus' body bare.

Nicodemus gasped. A strange feeling spread through his chest. He doubled over.

"What do you feel, Nicodemus?"

"Pain." He could not concentrate on words.

"Just pain?"

"No."

"What do you feel?" This time, Terrin's voice was sharper.

"It's...pulling me." Nicodemus whispered, stopping an inch away from the spells. "You have to let me go."

"Tell me how to put you back into your body and I'll remove the spells."

Nicodemus opened his mouth to tell him, and another wave of something dragged him even closer to the spell. His arm brushed the barrier and he fell back, a scream dying in his throat.

"Terrin, let me do it." Skade's voice was muffled by the door and the mirror, but Nicodemus could hear her clearly. "I know what I'm doing, and you'd likely kill him before you figured it out."

Nicodemus glanced up at the door. Terrin turned around.

"How do I know you're not planning something?" he snapped. "How do I know you won't try to escape?"

"I wouldn't leave Nicodemus alone with you even if you gave me back my beads and released me," Skade said. "Let me do it. I give you my word I won't try to escape."

Terrin hesitated.

"He's infected; did you know that? There's a good possibility he won't die from it, but it might be touch and go for a little while. I doubt you want to play nursemaid."

"No, I don't." Terrin glanced at Cathan, who shrugged.

Nicodemus held his breath. Skade would not let him die. She wouldn't cause him any undue pain. If Terrin let Skade reverse her spell, then he might have a chance to live through what was still to come.

"Very well." Terrin removed a key from his belt and gave it to Cathan. "Michael, release your mother and bring her to me."

Nicodemus sighed in relief and raised his head.

Cathan released Skade and stepped back. She pushed past him and strode directly to where Nicodemus' body lay. She ignored Terrin completely.

"I need some of my beads to do this," Skade said, and Nicodemus saw her walk through a cloud of freed magic and draw it into her body.

"I'm not giving you anything," Terrin snapped.

"Then you'll kill him," Skade said. "This spell was created with my magic; I need my beads to reverse it."

Terrin glowered at her. "No tricks."

"No tricks," she agreed, and held out her hand.

Terrin fished a strand of beads out of the bag and shoved them at Skade. She took them, broke the strand in half, and laid one piece across Nicodemus' mouth.

In the mirror, Nicodemus felt a strange coldness on his lips, but when he raised one hand to investigate, he felt nothing.

"Stand back," Skade ordered. "I don't want either of you to get in the way."

Nicodemus saw Enapay peek out from the doorway, and then duck back inside the room. No one else noticed her.

Skade pulled three of the beads from the broken strand and used some of the power she had collected to imbue them with a bright blue glow that spilled out of her clenched fist. She took the strand of beads away from his lips and gently opened his mouth. Then she positioned her hand over Nicodemus' mouth, hesitated, and looked up at him.

He could see what she could have done with the beads clearly in her eyes. He wanted to scream at her to leave him and stop Terrin and Cathan; to let him die, but his voice dried up in his throat.

"This might hurt a bit," Skade whispered, her face pale and strained. "I'm sorry, Nicodemus."

She dropped the first bead.

Nicodemus didn't see it fall, but he felt the mini explosion that knocked him back against Terrin's spells. Something hard and unyielding lodged in his throat.

He screamed.

"Your spells!" Skade's voice cut across the pain. "Drop them, Terrin. Drop them now."

The spells vanished. Nicodemus collapsed, choking.

"It won't be long now, Nicodemus. Hold on." Skade's voice whispered in his ear, but she still stood over his body on the other side of the mirror. He pulled himself up, using the mirror frame for support, and saw her drop the second bead.

The first bead burst into flame in his throat on contact with the second one. Nicodemus swallowed them both, allowing their heat to travel through the rest of his body. Even though his vision was blurry with tears, he saw the body on the table swallow in turn.

Terrin gasped. Skade ignored him and inserted the third bead between Nicodemus' lips.

The body on the table opened its eyes.

Quite suddenly, Nicodemus could see from both vantage points, a dizzying perspective. He swayed and pitched forward.

Skade put one hand on the body's arm, and Nicodemus felt her touch. He shuddered.

Thick lines of multi-colored magic twined out of the body's open mouth and swayed in the air for a moment in a hypnotizing display. Nicodemus glanced at Terrin, but both Cathan and Terrin paid no attention to the drifting strands of light.

"They can't see it," Skade whispered, somehow near his ear again. She glanced up at him and slowly lifted his body up. "Breathe, Nicodemus. Breathe."

A band of pure agony tightened around his throat. Nicodemus choked and gasped, but he could not seem to draw a breath. Blackness pressed down across his vision.

"Breathe!" Skade shouted, and crushed the remaining beads in her hand, raining shards of glowing power down over his head.

Nicodemus tried to push past the blockage, but he could not get a grip on it. The blackness blocked both sight and sound and drowned him in darkness. He fell forward against the mirror's glass.

He fell forward, but the glass was no longer there. Something grabbed him from the air and locked him in flesh before he could pull away.

Lungs expanded and contracted. The fire fled, only to be replaced by bone-numbing cold. Nicodemus opened his eyes and saw Skade's face above him, but it was blurry and strange.

He tasted blood in the back of his throat. For the first time in ten years, he smelled the acrid stench from the spell's destruction. For the first time in ten years, he felt the cramp of sudden hunger in his stomach.

He also felt something tear through his mind and burrow into his brain; eating away at whatever defenses he had left. He had no strength left to scream.

Skade smoothed down his hair. Her hand cooled his skin and gave him a little shred of comfort.

"Nicodemus, can you hear me?"

He tried to answer, but the thing burrowing in his brain destroyed all semblance of self-control. He felt his body shudder. Pain rippled up his chest. His sight dimmed, then vanished entirely, leaving him alone in darkness.

"What's happening to him?" he heard Terrin ask.

"This is your spell, Terrin." Nicodemus had only heard Skade so angry one other time. He stiffened and tried to shrink away from her before he realized she wasn't mad at him at all. "This is your spell."

"I thought you said he wouldn't die from it." Nicodemus could barely hear his voice.

"He might. He might not."

"Make sure he doesn't." Rough hands closed over Nicodemus' arms and legs.

"I'll carry him," Skade said, and the hands disappeared. Nicodemus felt her lift him up and cradle him to her breast.

He tried to speak to her, to tell her to leave him there and take Enapay and escape, but he couldn't force his mouth to form the words.

"Shhh," She lowered him down on a soft bed that cradled and comforted him. "Shhhh. Don't fight it, Nicodemus. Let it run its course."

He heard a footstep, then Terrin's voice. "Where is the girl?"

The girl. Enapay. Nicodemus remembered seeing her peek out of the open door while they were busy with his body, but he had not seen her leave.

She was well on her way to freeing her father. It had been Skade's idea for Enapay to slip out while Terrin and Cathan were distracted.

"Where is she?"

Even though the pain left him breathless with agony, Nicodemus was very glad he could not answer Terrin's question.

So, he sensed, was Skade, who lightly placed one finger over his lips before he gave in to darkness and let it carry him away.

Chapter 24

"Daddy? Daddy, can you hear me?"

Michael groaned and opened his eyes. He lay still for a moment, trying to remember what had happened, but his memories were sketchy at best. His mother had returned. He remembered having an argument with her in Enapay's bedroom, after...after someone had stolen his daughter away.

"Enapay?"

His daughter hurtled herself into his arms. Michael saw rope burns around his wrists, and the ropes that had bound him lying on the floor. Who had freed him? Enapay had just learned how to tie her shoes.

He pressed his face to Enapay's hair and held her tight. "I never thought I'd see you again."

"I missed you, daddy," she whispered. "I knew you weren't mean."

Cathan. Michael's heart sank. "What happened? Where are we?" If he had to guess, he'd say Leysan. Twenty-eight years ago, he could have named the castle from the stone used to build it. Now he wasn't so certain.

"Leysan," Enapay told him. "Nic-o-demus told me that."

That made sense with what little he knew. "What else did he tell you? How did you get here?"

"We can't stay here, daddy," Enapay said. "We have to go back for your mommy."

"My..." Michael stared at her. "My mother is here?"

A six-year-old's perception of things was not very reliable to begin with, but after a string of questions and Enapay's surprisingly detailed answers, Michael thought he knew what had happened.

Some questions remained, like how Enapay had managed to unlock the door to reach him, but he could worry about those questions later.

"Did my mother leave you with a plan?" he asked.

"She said get out of here as fast as you can." Enapay sounded like she had memorized Skade's words. "Get out of here and Find Help."

"Find help." Michael groaned. "If I'm recognized, I'll be killed."

"You could ask Espen for help," Enapay suggested.

Michael stared at her. "How do you know about Espen?" He realized that his daughter showed a maturity beyond her years, and saw the first glimmerings of the woman she would eventually become. The prospect frightened him more than he cared to admit.

He wasn't usually selfish, but he wished Sarah had not gone to England with Ivy and Jordan. He could have used her level-headed coolness right about now.

Enapay tugged on his hand. "We have to leave, daddy. They'll notice I'm gone."

Yes, they would notice, and Michael had no doubt Terrin would torture his daughter if he caught her again.

"I need a mirror." He had no idea if he could still use the mirror magic here, but he intended to try.

"We can look for one," Enapay said, and tugged on his hand again. "Come on."

She led him out of the room and into an empty corridor. Working from twenty-eight year old memories, Michael guessed they would have to pass through the sleeping quarters to reach the other flight of stairs if they wanted to avoid the room Terrin held Skade and the others in. Surely someone would have a mirror there.

The castle seemed to be empty. Michael discovered one of the reasons when he opened the council room door and found the bloated bodies of the council members still lying where they had died. He turned Enapay away from the sight, and continued on.

They found the first mirror in the second bedroom, but it had been smashed repeatedly with a heavy stone. The second and third mirrors were the same; the fourth and fifth were obviously missing from their places on the wall. By the time they reached the lower level of the castle, Michael was beginning to doubt they would ever find a mirror. And then when they reached the kitchen, he realized he did not need a mirror after all.

Any reflective surface could be made into a portal. Water worked best, but even blood would do in a pinch. Seers had used bowls of water for scrying for thousands of years. Skade had only improved on the effect.

Michael filled the largest bowl he could find with water and set it on the long empty table. Enapay climbed up on a stool and watched, solemn and silent.

"Do you have any idea where Espen is?" he asked. "I could put out a general call, but Terrin might hear it and know where we are."

"I don't know," Enapay whispered. "Skade didn't tell me."

"And neither did Nicodemus, I bet."

Enapay shook her head.

"Then if I tell you to run, run as fast as you can out of here, okay? I don't want him to catch you again."

"Okay." Her voice was very soft.

Michael nicked his finger with a sharp knife and dipped it into the water. One drop of his blood turned the water faintly pink.

"Say Espen's name, Enapay." He kept his gaze on the shimmering water. "Espen."

"Espen," Enapay echoed. "Espen!"

Something sucked at his makeshift portal and turned the water black. Michael gritted his teeth and sliced his finger a little deeper. The water turned a deep red.

"Espen!" His voice cracked; he tried again. "Espen!"

"Espen!" Enapay shouted.

The water shimmered. A face appeared, vanished, and appeared again.

"Michael." Espen's voice gave him nothing. "I should have known you'd show up. Where is your mother?"

"Enapay tells me she's being held prisoner here in Leysan," Michael said. He had no idea how much his mother had told her before Cathan severed the connection and brought her here. "How much did she tell you?"

"She claimed you were innocent," Espen said. "But from what I've been able to piece together after my mirror melted, you hit her over the head."

"It wasn't me." Michael glanced at Enapay, who smiled at him. "I swear to you, Espen. It wasn't me."

"She did say something about someone named Cathan 'putting on your face'," Espen allowed. "But since you very well could be that person, I'm sure you understand why I'm hesitant to help you."

"He's not!" Enapay piped up. "This is my real daddy."

A new face appeared beside Espen's, a pale smudge in the water.

"Who's that?" Michael asked.

"Zaira." Espen turned to glance at the little girl beside her. "You know I don't like to ask, but..."

"It's okay," Zaira whispered.

Michael remembered what Terrin had done to her and shivered. At least she was safe now, with Espen.

"Is this the real Michael?" Espen asked.

"Yes." Zaira stared through the mirror and Michael had to force himself not to look away from her gaze.

"Thank you." Espen smiled at Zaira and turned back to the mirror. Michael tried to remember how old the child had been when Terrin changed, her, but he had trouble reconciling what he saw in the mirror with what he remembered from before. He had to keep in mind that only ten years had passed here, not twenty-eight.

What would Sarah do in this situation? He had no patience for planning or plots. He had no idea how to get his mother away from Terrin, other than bursting into the room and hoping no one killed him before he managed to free her.

He wished he had a gun, or some sort of weapon, but guns did not exist here and it had been twenty-eight years since he had touched a proper sword. He had his magic, but how good would that be here?

"What do you want me to do, Michael?"

Michael stared at his daughter and made up his mind. "Take Enapay. Keep her safe."

"Daddy?" Enapay whispered.

Michael couldn't look at her for fear he would break down and cry. "I want you to go with Espen, Enapay. Do you think you can do that? You'll be safe there, until I can come for you."

"Michael, what are you planning to do?" Espen leaned forward and the picture in the mirror strengthened enough for him to make out the expression on her face.

"I'm not sure, but I'm not going to leave my mother here," Michael said. "Will you take Enapay and keep her safe? If I... If I don't succeed, her mother will be back from England in a little less than a week, our time."

"Of course I'll take her." Espen didn't question his decision. "Will she fit through whatever you're using?"

"A bowl of water. I think she'll fit." Michael turned to Enapay. "It's only for a little while. You'll be safe with Espen."

"I don't want to go, Daddy," Enapay whispered. "I want to stay here and help you!"

For a moment, he was tempted to let her stay. She had untied him, after all, and no normal six-year-old would have been able to do that. But if she stayed and Terrin killed her, Michael would never be able to forgive himself for putting his daughter in danger.

She's been in danger since she was born, he thought. She obviously knows how to take care of herself, but she's only six... And 'only six' was the deciding factor. If Terrin didn't kill him, Sarah would if he put his daughter in danger purposely.

"I'll come for you as soon as I can. I promise."

Enapay threw her arms around him and hugged him tight.

"I love you, Daddy."

Michael blinked back tears. "I love you too, honey." Then he lifted her over the bowl of water, strengthened the portal as much as he could, and lowered her through it.

He felt someone take hold of her on the other side, and then she was gone.

Chapter 25

"Now," Espen said as soon as Michael had closed the portal and Enapay was safe on her lap. "Show me what you can do."

The vampire hesitated.

Espen softened the tone of her voice. "I'm not going to hurt you. Surely you know that by now."

"I know," the vampire whispered. "I just..."

"Can you help my daddy?" Enapay whispered, on the verge of tears.

"I hope so." The vampire picked up a small knife from the counter and pressed it against the edge of his thumb. He wiped blood across the mirror, and spoke Alban's name.

The mirror shimmered, then showed the familiar iron cage. Espen gasped.

"There's no mirror in that room," Zaira said smugly. "And we saw Nicodemus too."

"Show me." Espen's voice held a tone the vampire didn't quite trust. He stared at her warily for a moment, then spoke Nicodemus' name.

But this time, instead of seeing him inside the mirror, they saw him lying on a small bed with Skade bending over him, her face set and grim.

"Oh, no," Espen whispered.

For once, Zaira asked the question. "What happened? Why is he in color?"

"He's alive," Enapay said. "I escaped while they were doing the spell."

The vampire felt coldness settle into his stomach. "Alive?"

"He never died," Espen explained. "Skade took his spirit out of his body, more for punishment than any desire to keep him aware. She hid his body somewhere in Iomar. I assume Terrin found it."

"Nicodemus told him where it was and how to get past Skade's spells," Enapay said. "Terrin hurt him a lot."

"I can imagine he did." Espen stared at the scene in the mirror for a long moment, then sighed and glanced at the vampire. "Can you do a proper portal?"

"I don't know."

"Can he do a proper portal, Zaira?"

Zaira blinked. "Yes. But I don't think he knows how."

"Good. I think I can teach him." Espen lowered Enapay to the floor and stood. "Zaira, will you find Enapay something to eat and drink? We might be a while."

"I'm not hungry," Enapay said, and crossed her arms in front of her chest. For a moment, she looked so much like Skade that the vampire blinked in amazement.

"But I bet you're tired," Espen said. "What if Zaira tells you a story and I let you sleep with Jess?"

"Who's Jess?" Enapay asked. The vampire thought she looked tired, but if she was anything like her grandmother, she would never admit it.

"My cat. She's around here somewhere. Zaira, where's Jess?"

Zaira smiled. "I know where to look." She held out her hand. "Do you want to come with me, Enapay?"

Enapay stared at her for a moment, sensing she was being left out of things, but she finally took Zaira's hand and allowed her to lead her out of the room.

"I never asked you what your name was," Espen said as soon as they were gone.

The vampire stared at her. "No, you didn't."

"Do you mind if I do?"

"It doesn't feel like my name," the vampire whispered. "I feel no connection to it at all."

Espen glanced at him. "I imagine after so many years without a name, having one would feel strange."

"It's Alexander," the vampire said.

"Do you have any idea who your mother was?"

The vampire shook his head. "I don't remember ever having a mother. Terrin said... Terrin said Alban and I were twins."

"Show me your brother again."

The vampire spoke Alban's name and the mirror shimmered and showed the silent figure in the iron cage.

"You made him into a vampire; have you tried to contact him?"

"No. I..." He had not thought to try. "How can I do that?"

"I've seen it done, but I never thought to ask," Espen admitted. "Try touching the mirror, to start with. If you can see him, you should be able to speak to him as well."

"I can see the spell," the vampire whispered. "I'm not sure that I can break it."

"If anyone can, it's you," Espen said. "Go slowly. Don't hurt him. If you can break that spell, Terrin will lose most of his advantage."

The vampire made the mirror's view move closer to his brother's face. Alban's eyes were half-open, but unaware. A thin stream of bloody drool slipped down the side of his face.

He saw the spell as a twisting thing that wove in and out through Alban's mind, trapping him with no hope that he would ever become aware enough to break the spell himself. He started with the easy parts, the pieces he could see, in the hope that he wiped enough of it away to allow his brother to free himself.

Three hours later, he was still at it, determined to succeed.

Chapter 26

"Nicodemus, can you hear me?"

Skade's voice brought him back from the darkness in slow stages. He fought the whole time, wanting oblivion, but she would not let him go.

"Wake him up," Terrin said impatiently. "I want to know where that little brat went."

"Give him time!" Skade sounded as if she struggled to keep a tight reign on her temper. "How do you think you would feel if you were forced back into your body after ten years as a ghost?"

"She has a point," Cathan said, still using Michael's voice. Nicodemus wondered if Skade knew Michael was free and not a traitor. Surely Enapay had told her. If not, he resolved to tell her as soon as he figured out how to open his eyes.

He felt something enveloping part of his mind, and probed at the covering for a moment before he realized what Skade had done.

He felt no pain. He knew he was still infected; he could feel the sickness eating away at him if he tried hard enough, but the horrible pain was gone. Skade had found a way to block it somehow.

Nicodemus almost sighed in relief, then remembered Terrin and Cathan's presence. He would have to wait until they left to thank Skade for her kindness.

"I don't care about his comfort," Terrin snapped. "Nicodemus, where did the brat go?"

It was a question, and he had to answer. He struggled to keep his mouth closed, but he could no longer pretend he was unconscious.

"She's...not here." He felt his eyes begin to open and saw a blurry sliver of light. He blinked and tried to make the blurs come into focus.

"What's wrong with his eyes?" Cathan gasped.

"My eyes?" He raised one hand and tried to find his face, but Skade took his hand and held it before he could figure out which way to aim. His sense of direction had been destroyed. He felt like a stranger in his own body, and he did not like the feeling.

"Shhh. Don't worry about it, Nicodemus." Her voice was soft and soothing. "I'm sure it will go away soon."

No vision had come to him at Cathan's question. He did not know the answer! He groped for his face again, and Skade caught that hand as well.

"She's not here. Where did she go?" Terrin didn't seem to be disturbed about the state of Nicodemus' eyes.

Again this was information Nicodemus already knew. No new vision arrived with the question.

"She went...to free her father," he whispered.

Nicodemus heard Terrin curse. Skade's grip on his hands tightened.

"Her father is right here behind me," Terrin struggled to fill in the holes of doubt his lapse might have caused. Again, Nicodemus wondered if Skade knew her son was no traitor.

Even if she didn't know, Skade asked no questions.

"Can you see me?" Terrin asked abruptly.

Nicodemus tried to focus on the blur of color in front of him, but it remained a blur.

"N-no." He felt a tear slip down the side of his cheek. "I can't see any of you."

"Pity." Terrin dismissed his blindness easily. "Where is Enapay now, Nicodemus?"

Again, no vision appeared to show him the answer to the question. He knew where she had gone, but not where she was now.

He came very close to admitting he did not know, but a new thought intruded before he could give his ignorance away. Terrin would believe whatever he said. If he couldn't dream the answer, then he could lie.

"She's..." He cast around for possible places for a six-year-old child to go. Skade's grip tightened on his hands. "She's still in the castle. In the pantry, hiding."

"Go get her," Terrin ordered. Nicodemus assumed he spoke to Cathan, since Skade was a prisoner.

He had to lie again, so soon. "If you don't hurry she'll get away."

The blow literally came out of nowhere, backed by power and stunning force. Nicodemus heard Skade cry out, and then his head rang with the repercussions of Terrin's fist. He tasted blood--tasted!--in the back of his throat and almost choked. Something wet and thick and heavy ran across the top of his lip and down the side of his cheek.

"Was that necessary?" Skade asked. Nicodemus could hardly hear her voice.

"I want him to know what will happen if he lies to me," Terrin said. "Fix his eyes. I don't want to be forced to look at him like that." He slammed the door behind him.

Nicodemus swallowed blood. He felt Skade gently wipe the side of his face and hold a soft cloth under his nose. The pain receded quickly; Skade's block still held in place.

"He's gone," Skade said after a moment. "I'm sorry I didn't stop him in time. I didn't see it coming."

"What's wrong with my eyes?" Nicodemus asked.

Skade's ministrations ceased. "Don't you know? He asked you a question."

Should he tell her? Would she bother to try to save him if he was worthless? He could not keep it a secret for long.

"I can't...see anymore," he whispered. "I can't see anything."

"Oh." Skade's voice trailed off. "Then that part about Enapay in the pantry?"

"You know that isn't your son, don't you?" Nicodemus asked. "Did Enapay tell you?"

"Yes, she did. Is he free?"

"I made that part about Enapay up," Nicodemus whispered. "As far as I know, she is safe. But I can't see."

Skade sighed. "Your eyes are...well, they look like they're swimming in blood. Can you see anything at all?"

"Light. Colors. But they don't move."

"I'm going to wave my hand in front of your eyes," Skade said. A moment passed. "Did you see anything?"

The white light remained white; the colors blurry and soft. No shadow appeared across his vision; no way of knowing if she had waved her hand in front of his eyes or not.

"I didn't see anything," Nicodemus whispered. "I didn't see anything at all."

Chapter 27

For the first time in a long time, Alban opened his eyes and remembered. He had not been entirely oblivious over the past few months; he knew time had passed, but he did not know how much time. He knew he had been under the spell again, and he felt its path across every nerve in his body.

He opened his eyes. Sight was slow to return, but painless, a gradual sharpening of the bars that surrounded him. His father had not wanted him to escape this time. He almost wept in despair.

"Alban, can you hear me?"

The voice sounded familiar, but it took him a long moment to place it. He glanced around, but as far as he could tell, he was the only one in the room.

"Don't try to get up. The spell is still there."

If the spell was still there, then how could he be aware of his surroundings? He opened his mouth to ask, and ran his tongue across parched lips.

"Where are you?" His voice cracked.

"In..." He sensed the vampire's confusion. "I'm not sure."

"Nearby," a new voice said. Alban didn't recognize this voice at all. It soothed his tired mind and promised him peace. He felt tears gather in his eyes. "That's all you need to know. We're not far away, and I won't leave you there for much longer, Alban."

"I..." He tried to remember what had happened to him, but memory was slow to surface. "You're my brother."

"Yes. Do you remember my name?"

Alban concentrated hard. "Alexander."

"I've given you your mind back, Alban, but I can't go any farther. You're going to have to do that yourself."

Alban remembered another spell, and Kyne's aid. His throat worked, but he could not force himself to utter the words.

"Don't leave me alone..." He managed to lift one hand and held it out, supplicating. "Please don't leave me alone..."

He heard the vampire, Alexander, sigh. "I won't leave you alone. Espen tells me I can use this mirror until you are free."

"How is it that you can see me?" Alban asked. "I thought..." He struggled with the memories. "I thought you had to have a mirror on both sides to make it work." He knew no such thing, but that made sense.

"The spell Terrin created used my power as well as yours," the vampire said. "I'm not sure why I can see you, though. Espen thinks it's because we're related."

"You won't leave me?" Alban asked. He had to make sure he would not be alone.

"No. I'll stay here. But you have to break the spell again, Alban, and it won't be as easy this time."

Alban remembered the pain from the last breaking and wondered if he would survive this time. Wondered if he wanted to survive.

And decided that he did. He closed his eyes, pushed away weariness and the lagging effects of the spell, and tried to find the pieces left intact.

A memory drifted to the forefront of his mind. He remembered how Terrin had caught him, and realized he did not know the answer to the question he had wanted to ask Skade's mirror.

The vampire, Alexander, was with Espen. If Alban's memories were correct, so was Teluride, and so was Zaira, Terrin's Dreamer. She would know the answer.

"I have a question to ask Zaira," Alban whispered. "Is she there?"

"I'm here."

"Did I kill..." Alban could not continue. He closed his eyes. "Before, when I was in Iomar, my father told me I murdered King Valdis on his order. I intended to ask Skade's mirror if this was true, but I never got a chance." So much speaking exhausted him, but he wanted to know the truth. "Did I kill him, Zaira?"

Zaira didn't answer for the longest time. Alban did not ask again; he wasn't certain he could find enough strength to venture the question once more.

"No." He almost missed her whisper. "No, you didn't kill him. Terrin tried to make you do it, but you refused. That's what broke the spell in the first place."

Alban covered his face with his hands and wept in relief.

Chapter 28

"He's gone," Cathan said, slipping empty-handed into the room. Terrin turned. "What do you mean, he's gone?"

"Michael's gone. And so is the girl. I found a bowl of bloody water in the kitchen, but I couldn't find any sign of Michael or the brat."

Terrin felt the fine strands of his careful plan slipping away. He clenched his teeth and closed his eyes. "Where did you look?"

"I searched the entire castle." Cathan did not move from his place beside the door, as if he expected Terrin to strike out at him. "We smashed all the mirrors, remember?"

"How could I forget?" Terrin turned towards the last mirror in the castle and ran his finger down the smooth glass. "They won't stay away for long."

"Michael could have returned to his home," Cathan said. "If you wish, I can..."

"No." Terrin held up one hand and Cathan fell silent. "No. Michael didn't leave. He wouldn't leave his mother a prisoner."

Cathan glanced towards the closed door. "Is she truly a prisoner? Surely someone as powerful as Skade..."

Terrin shook his head. "He wouldn't leave his mother here. Not if the brat told him what happened. He's still here in the castle, and we're going to set a trap for him."

He stroked the bag full of Skade's beads. He had not destroyed them yet; more of a precaution than anything else. If the beads had brought Nicodemus back to life, then perhaps they could be used to cure him of the sickness before he died.

If he died. Remembering Nicodemus' eyes, Terrin was not sure death would be such a bad thing. What use could a blind dreamer be, if only an object to be used? He frowned and looked towards the door where Skade and Nicodemus waited for him. Nicodemus' answers had not been very helpful. Perhaps he needed a little persuasion to remind him who his master was now.

"Bring Nicodemus to me," he ordered, and turned back to the mirror. Cathan, relieved to not be on the end of Terrin's anger, hurried to open the door.

"Absolutely not!" Terrin heard Skade protest as Cathan attempted to do his bidding, and he realized he would have to bring her down a peg or two if he wanted to gain her respect. No, not her respect. He wanted Skade, high and mighty Skade, to fear him.

He clutched the bag and pulled power from his son. The connection didn't seem to be as strong as before, but he had not fed Alban in a while, and even vampires weakened eventually.

The velvet began to burn. The beads inside, to melt.

He heard Skade gasp. A moment later, Cathan dragged Nicodemus out of the room and deposited him at Terrin's feet.

"I hope that hurt, my lady," Terrin said softly. "There's more to come."

Cathan glanced up at him. "Do you want me to bring her out to watch?"

"No. Guard the door and let her wonder what I'm doing to her ghost." He kicked Nicodemus and was pleased to hear him moan. Terrin crouched down beside him. "Nicodemus, I have a question for you."

"Leave me alone." Nicodemus' horrible eyes flickered open and he tried to rise, but ten years of weightlessness had made their mark. He had no sense of balance left without sight to help him.

Terrin laughed. "I didn't put you back into your body to leave you alone. I have a question for you."

"I have no answers." Nicodemus managed to get to his knees, but he held himself stiffly, as if expecting an attack from every angle.

Terrin waved his hand in front of his prisoner's face and received no reaction at all. He frowned. The spell had changed Zaira, but what would it do to Nicodemus? He certainly didn't seem to be in any pain...

He found Skade's spell a moment later, and realized what she had done. Had he been wrong about the beads? Constructing a spell like the one she had placed over Nicodemus to keep the pain at bay took enormous reserves of power. Skade should have been helpless.

He crushed the velvet bag to his chest and felt beads shatter from the heat. Tiny flakes of glass drifted down over Nicodemus and sparkled on the floor where they fell.

He felt the power that remained in the beads, but it was nothing like the power that held the pain from the sickness at bay. What would happen if he severed that spell and sent its power back to Skade? Would she fear him then?

Terrin hesitated, only because he needed Nicodemus' visions to help his plan succeed. If Skade's spell was the only thing keeping Nicodemus conscious and sane, then breaking it would not be a good idea.

But he could experiment without breaking the spell. He could test it and see how powerful Skade truly was without her precious beads, and force Nicodemus to answer his questions at the same time.

He settled one hand on Nicodemus' bowed head. He could feel Skade's spell throbbing under his touch. Very gently, he tweaked it, just enough to get her attention. Nicodemus gasped and doubled over.

"Terrin!" He saw her shadow under the door and smiled. "Terrin, he is nothing to you. Don't hurt him."

"Ah, but he is everything to me," Terrin said. "Without Nicodemus to answer my questions, my plan would be lost."

Nicodemus sobbed quietly against the floor. Terrin grabbed a handful of his hair and pulled him up. "Where is Skade's son, Nicodemus?"

"I don't know." The words were torn out of his throat.

"What do you mean, you don't know?" Terrin redoubled his grip on Nicodemus' hair. His prisoner gasped and tried to struggle away, but a dagger pressed against his throat soon stopped his struggles.

"I don't know. I can't see. I can't see anything." Blood streamed down Nicodemus' chin and dripped on Terrin's hand.

That presented a problem. If Nicodemus couldn't answer his questions, then he had no value as a prisoner. And if he had no value as a prisoner, then Terrin had wasted his time forcing him back into his body. He growled under his breath.

"You can't tell me where Skade's son is?"

"N-no." Nicodemus' eyes leaked blood now, as if the sickness had suddenly gotten worse. Terrin twitched Skade's spell again. "No, please..."

What if Skade's spell prevented him from dreaming? If he tore it away, would Nicodemus go mad from the pain? Did he care? Without his talent, Nicodemus was nothing.

"Terrin, please!" Skade pounded on the door. Terrin ignored her.

Nicodemus opened his eyes as Terrin took hold of the spell. Blood masked the lower half of his face. The look in his blind eyes almost made Terrin pause.

But he had to know. He had to know if Nicodemus' talent was lost to him, or if Skade had hidden it under her spell.

He tore the spell away and heard Skade scream. A moment later, Nicodemus collapsed under the onslaught of the sickness, eerily silent, as if he had forgotten how to voice his pain. His body shook with convulsions. His eyes ran red with blood. Terrin stepped away from him.

"Nicodemus, where is Michael?"

Nicodemus moaned, a lost, strangling sound.

Terrin backed his question with power and aimed it at Nicodemus' unprotected body. "Nicodemus, where is Michael? Answer me, damn you!"

"I'm right here." The voice came from behind him, towards the door. Terrin had been so intent upon torturing his prisoner that he had not heard Skade's son approach. And where was Cathan? He saw a sprawled figure outside the door, and realized he would not be able to count on him for backup.

Terrin unsheathed his dagger and pressed it against Nicodemus' throat. "I'll kill him if you step inside this room."

Michael held a metal bar in one hand. His other hand held a glowing ball of light that hurt Terrin's eyes to look at it.

"Put your weapons down or Nicodemus dies."

Michael let the metal pole clatter to the floor. The ball of light hovered in the air for a moment and cast strange shadows over his face.

"That too," Terrin snapped.

Almost in slow motion, Terrin saw Michael grab the ball of light and gently toss it towards the locked door that Skade stood behind. He heard Michael yell something, and saw him dive out of the way.

The dagger bit into Nicodemus' throat as a convulsion rippled through his body. Terrin moved the blade away. He did not want to cut Nicodemus' throat too soon.

When the glowing ball hit the door, the explosion knocked him off his feet and against the wall. He hit his head on the edge of the mirror and felt blackness rise up to claim him. Only by pulling power from the spell over Alban did he manage to push the darkness back.

Across the room, the door now lay in smoking splinters. Terrin didn't see Skade anywhere, but Nicodemus lay unmoving in the middle of the floor, scratched and bloody from the debris. He did not see Michael anywhere.

Terrin used the mirror's frame to help him rise, and slowly staggered over to where Nicodemus lay. He had dropped his dagger, but that didn't matter anymore.

He pulled on the spell, but he couldn't find the link. He frowned, swayed, and cast his mind out to where his son had been imprisoned since the vampire did his bidding one last time. Alban was gone.

Gone! Fury stole his voice. He was gone!

Had Michael stolen him away? Terrin forgot about Nicodemus and turned towards the door. Had Michael done this to him? He could think of no one else.

He could think of no one else he would like to kill, and he knew just how to do it.

Chapter 29

Skade had not been quick enough to heed Michael's shout before the door exploded. She lay on her side under the broken bed for a long moment, testing each and every bone for breakage and realizing that she was getting too old for this. She had allowed herself to be tricked by a stripling as old as her son.

She bit back a groan and slowly rose to her knees, aches and pains making her progress slow. She had to use a long thin piece from the bed to help her stand. Only then did she stagger out of the room.

The first thing she saw was Nicodemus, lying silent and still in the middle of the path of destruction. The second thing she saw was Terrin, standing right over the spot where he had destroyed the rest of her beads. The shards still sparkled with magic; magic she could use? She had no idea, but she intended to try.

The third thing she saw was her son, staring at her from the doorway. A thin stream of blood ran down his face from a cut on his scalp, but he seemed to be largely unhurt.

"You stole my son as well?" Terrin asked. He faced Michael, and had not seen her yet. Skade slowly moved out of the doorway, towards Nicodemus.

"I had nothing to do with your son's disappearance," Michael said. Skade saw his eyes flicker towards her once, but Terrin did not notice.

"You lie very well," Terrin said. "Too well, in fact. Who else could have freed him? Did you have a chance to send him to the same place you sent your daughter?"

"I hope he's far away from here." Michael stepped back as Terrin advanced. Skade called to the shards of glass that littered the floor and they rose, winking in the dim light.

Terrin spun around. "What..." He threw up his hands, and Skade ducked as something shattered against the wall at her back. He shouted out a string of syllables, and Skade felt something prick her skin. When she glanced down at her arm, she saw beads of blood from some unknown source, staining the sleeve of her gown a deep purple.

"Mother!" Michael ran into the room, and Terrin turned on him, snarling. Before Skade could stop him, Terrin threw her son against the wall. Michael collapsed, unmoving.

When Skade told the shards of glass to attack, something alien rippled up her spine at the first spark of power. As the shining motes sank into Terrin's skin, pain spread across her skin and burrowed into her flesh.

She knew at once what Terrin had done.

Coldness seized her heart and nearly stopped her lungs. She saw the rows of beds deep down under the castle; remembered the screams of the dying as the sickness sucked them dry.

Skade knew that the only way to postpone the inevitable was to stop using magic, but she could not allow Terrin to kill both her son and Nicodemus. If she had to sacrifice herself to save them both, she would.

She clenched her teeth against the pain and ordered the shards to dig deeper. She felt them tear through muscle and bore their way deep into Terrin's skin. The pain must have been excruciating, but he did not stop.

He left a trail of blood across the floor.

Skade sank to her knees beside Nicodemus and rolled him over. His eyes were closed. Blood leaked out from under his eyelids and crusted across his eyelashes, preventing her from seeing whatever damage Terrin had done.

Skade felt the pain dig deeper as she drew breath to whisper a spell. She watched Terrin pick up a dagger and knew he meant to kill them all.

Skade couldn't let that happen. She flung out her hand towards the mirror, and poured the rest of her power into creating a portal.

The mirror flickered wildly for a moment, distracting Terrin. He turned around just as Michael opened his eyes. Skade saw her son lift something up from the floor and throw it at Terrin to knock him off balance, but she no longer had the strength to help him. She could not hear Terrin's shout of rage. She barely felt Nicodemus stir under her hand. She saw him open his eyes, felt a faint glimmer of amazement when she realized that his eyes were only bloodshot, not red.

Terrin completed his turn and came for her, dagger raised to thrust. Skade knew she did not have enough strength to avoid him, so she stayed where she was, kneeling over Nicodemus, who mouthed a question she did not hear.

Michael launched himself from the floor as Terrin reached her. She saw him scream something, but she could not hear his voice.

Skade saw the dagger flash. She closed her eyes and tensed for pain, but someone pushed her out of the way. Sound returned with a short, choked scream that did not come from her throat. When she opened her eyes, she saw Nicodemus bent low in the midst of the debris, blood staining his hands.

She struggled to rise, but blackness hovered on the edge of her vision. She could barely feel the scraps of wood beneath her.

Terrin jerked the dagger out of Nicodemus' chest and vanished into the portal. It rippled, but held, a testament to her power. Nicodemus sank to the floor. Skade crawled to him and tried to staunch the blood, but her hands shook too wildly to be of much use. She could not save him this time.

This time, he would die.

Skade forgot about her son, who gently lifted her hands away from Nicodemus' body a moment later.

"I have to help him." She hardly recognized her own voice.

"Mother, I..." Michael's voice was thick with tears. "Do you realize what Terrin did to you?"

Skade managed to smile at him. "Yes. I know what he did." She pulled strength from somewhere and felt the pain recede a little bit. "I know what he did, but I still have to help him." She caught her son's arm. "If we are to live--all of us--you must contact Espen through the mirror and bring her here."

Michael opened his mouth to speak, but Skade shook her head.

"Please, Michael. I have little enough strength as it is."

With one last look back at her, Michael moved to do her bidding. Skade watched him for a moment, weary to the bone, then sighed and dropped her gaze.

Nicodemus coughed. Bright blood dotted his lips. His eyes were wide and filled with pain from both the spell and the wound.

Skade stroked the side of his face. "I never realized you'd turn out the way you did. I thought I'd have to leave you in the mirror until I died."

Nicodemus tried to smile. "You will never die."

"I'm dying now." Skade took his hand. "And so are you." Pain caught at her throat and closed it. She forced it away. "Nicodemus, is there any way I can save your life?"

He stared at her, astonishment overriding the pain for a moment before it returned. "Skade, I was meant to die."

"That's not what I asked," Skade whispered. She swayed and caught herself against a twisted chunk of wood.

"Sometimes, it's best not to ask." Nicodemus closed his eyes. "I would rather see you live, my Queen."

Tears spilled down Skade's cheeks. She wiped her face with one shaking hand and tried to think. How could she save him? How could she make sure he did not die because of her?

The answer arrived quickly enough, so obvious that she did not think it would work at first. "Nicodemus, if I..."

He turned his face away. "No."

"If there is a way to save your life, don't you want me to save it?" Skade asked.

For a moment, she thought he would refuse again, but he opened his eyes and turned his face towards her again.

"There is one way," he whispered. "Put me back in the mirror."

"That will work?" She had to make sure before she tried. She doubted she had enough strength for a second attempt.

His eyes glittered with unshed tears. "I might not remember you."

Skade's hand closed over his. "I'll take that chance."

She had no beads, no magic, and only enough strength to cover one hand with Nicodemus' blood and stagger to the mirror.

Michael turned at her approach. "Mother?" He caught her as she fell against him, and held her close. "Mother, I...I don't want you to die."

Pain and exhaustion ate away at Skade's tiny reserve of strength. She closed her eyes and leaned against her son, careful not to smear any of Nicodemus' blood on his clothes.

"Help me to the mirror."

Michael stared down at her. She had not realized he had grown so tall in ten years. He could have forced her to lie down, but he did as she asked and helped her to the mirror.

Skade placed her bloody hand against the glass and whispered Nicodemus' name. The portal shimmered and Espen's face swam into view.

"Skade! What happened?"

Behind her, Nicodemus moaned. Skade gripped the edge of the mirror's frame and stared through her bloody handprint at Espen.

"I have to do one last thing before I come to you," she whispered. She could not stop crying. "Michael, carry Nicodemus to the mirror."

Michael did as she asked again. Skade stared down at Nicodemus' face and gave him a trembling smile. "If you don't remember me, at least remember that I didn't hate you this time."

Nicodemus' lips twitched. "I will." He gasped softly and tensed in Michael's arms.

Skade stepped away from the mirror, barely able to stand upright on her own. She felt disconnected from both her body and the pain, and numbness invaded her fingers and toes. She gripped the edge of the frame and clenched her teeth. She would see this through, and then allow herself to collapse.

At her whispered instructions, Michael lay Nicodemus on the table Terrin had used to force him back into his body. He made sure the reflection was of Nicodemus alone, then gently took her arm and pulled her away from the mirror.

Skade wanted to close her eyes and give into the pain, but she could not leave Nicodemus alone to die. She caught his gaze, held it, and smiled at him.

"I'm very proud of what you did for me."

His fingers twitched. He tried to smile, but life faded quickly from his eyes. "Thank you, Skade." And then, he died.

Michael's strong arms were the only things that kept her upright. Skade felt him lift her, but she didn't have enough strength to protest. She heard Espen's voice murmur something, and Michael's voice reply.

"Sleep," Espen whispered in her ear. "You're safe. Michael's safe. No one will harm you here."

Skade let out her breath in a long sigh, released her hold on grief and pain and let the darkness rise to carry her away.

The End

Cast of Characters

Terrin

Wants only one thing: to rule Leysan and to destroy Skade for meddling in his plans previously. He thinks he can succeed, but only if he murders all competitors for the throne.

Skade

Michael's mother, Queen of Iomar. Tends to stick her nose where it doesn't belong.

Espen

one of the order of Healers

Zaira

a child prophet.

Alban

Terrin's son. Alexander's twin.

Alexander (the vampire)

Terrin's son. Alban's twin. Has more courage than he thinks.

Teluride

heir to the throne of Leysan. Poisoned by Terrin. Recuperating in Espen's house.

Nicodemus (the Ghost in Skade's mirror)

a prophet. Michael's friend. He was imprisoned in Skade's mirror after he contracted the virus Terrin, Michael, and Cathan helped create.

Michael

Skade's son. He was exiled for his part in the scandal that involved Nicodemus, Cathan, and Terrin.

Enapay

Michael's six-year-old daughter.

Cathan

Terrin's friend. A shapeshifter who can mimic anyone; including Skade's son, Michael.

You can find ALL our books up on our website at:

http://www.writers-exchange.com

All Jennifer's books:

http://www.writers-exchange.com/Jennifer-St-Clair/

all our fantasy novels:

http://www.writers-exchange.com/category/genres/fantasy/

About the Author

J ennifer St. Clair grew up in Southern Ohio and spent most of her childhood in the woods around her home. She wrote her first novel when she was thirteen, and hasn't stopped since. She lives with her ball python, Fester, and two cats, Ash and Rowan.

In her spare time, she crochets, makes cloth dolls, collects antiques, books, and vintage clothing, and takes digital photographs with varying degrees of success.

Her *Beth-Hill series* is set in the area in America that contains many supernatural creatures: Wild Hunt, Vampires, Dragons, Faery and more.

It is part of the Universe that her *Jacob Lane Series, Karen Montgomery Series* and vampire trilogy, *The Shadow Series* are set in.

Follow all her books on her author page:

http://www.writers-exchange.com/Jennifer-St-Clair/

If you want to read more about other books by this author, they are listed on the following pages...

A Beth-Hill Novel (Stand Alone Novels)

Are creatures of the night and all manner of extramundane beings drawn to certain locations in the natural world? In the Midwestern village of Beth-Hill located in southern Ohio, the population is made up of its fair share of common citizens...and much more than its share of supernatural residents. Take a walk on the wild side in this unusual place where imagination meets reality.

Blood of Innocents

Ten years ago, Orien, crown prince of the Seleighe, was captured by his mortal enemies, locked in a dungeon and turned into a vampire. Six years into Orien's sentence, the Healer's brother Cullen disobeyed his mistress's orders to kill him and turned him into a vampire instead, thus sealing both their fates for all eternity.

Now both Orien and Cullen are set free. But a secret only Cullen knows lies locked inside his mind, threatening to drive him mad before he can uncover the identity of a traitor--the very elf who betrayed Orien and left them both to die in darkness.

Publisher: http://www.writers-exchange.com/blood-of-innocents/

Full Moon

Werewolves change into wolves when the moon is full. But Edward's curse only allows him to be *human* when the moon is full.

Alone and despairing, Edward hides himself away from the world. He's scraped out a meager existence for himself for almost a century in the forest he's grown to love and call home. But in the depths of a terrible winter, he stumbles across clues from the life his mother left behind in Faerie. The truth may give him the answers he needs about the source of his birthright... and the curse that holds him captive.

Publisher: http://www.writers-exchange.com/full-moon/

A Beth-Hill Novel: Jacob Lane Series

Are creatures of the night and all manner of extramundane beings drawn to certain locations in the natural world? In the Midwestern village of Beth-Hill located in southern Ohio, the population is made up of its fair share of common citizens...and much more than its share of supernatural residents.

Jacob Lane is a ten-year-old girl who's spent her life unaware of her magical heritage. After being sent to Darkbrook, a school of magic, supernatural mysteries seem to spring to life all around her and her new friends.

Book 1: The Tenth Ghost

After Jacob Lane's parents mysteriously vanish, she's sent to Darkbrook, the only school of magic in the United States. While there, she and her new friends stumble upon a series of mysterious deaths in the nine ghosts that haunt the halls of Darkbrook. These ghosts were students who died at the school over the past hundred years. Will Jacob become the tenth ghost, or can she stop a witch's reign of terror?

Publisher: http://www.writers-exchange.com/the-tenth-ghost/

Book 2: The Ninth Guest

When Jacob's friend Ophelia's family decides to open up their castle for guests, amateur paranormal sleuth Jacob Lane is invited to join in on the fun. "Spend the night in a vampire's castle and live to tell the tale!" is supposed to be a fundraiser to help Ophelia's family pay the bills. Heating a castle costs quite a bit, after all. But, after the truth of an old secret is uncovered, what began as an innocent business venture soon turns deadly when vampire hunters get involved.

For years, the vampire hunters have had only one goal: To destroy all vampires. With the help of a new friend, Jacob and Ophelia must work together to save the entire VonBriggle family from extinction.

Publisher: http://www.writers-exchange.com/the-ninth-guest/

Book 3: The Eighth Room

For two hundred years, the Selkies have kept themselves separate from those who live on land. But now the Selkies need allies or they'll be crushed by their ancient enemies, the Finfolk.

Jacob and Ophelia, students at the only school of magic in the United States, uncover a mystery that dates back to Darkbrook's beginnings. While helping clean out old storage rooms for classroom expansion, they find something that might save the Selkies from extinction. With the help of the youngest member of the Wild Hunt who are no longer so wild or terrifying, they must foil the Finfolk who desire the Selkie's destruction...or die trying.

Publisher: http://www.writers-exchange.com/the-eighth-room/

Book 4: The Seventh Secret

After a picture of Niklas, the dragons' liaison to the only school of magic in the United States, shows up in too many newspapers to count, Darkbrook is forced to go on the defensive. The secret of Darkbrook's existence has been discovered. But there are more than dragonhunters in the forest, and, as Jacob Lane, supernatural sleuth and student at Darkbrook, learns how to use her newly discovered talent of healing, she helps to right an old wrong and must battle a teenaged wizard intent on proving--once and for all--that magic is real.

Publisher: http://www.writers-exchange.com/the-seventh-secret/

Book 5: The Sixth Stone

Jacob Lane, supernatural sleuth, and Danny, her werewolf friend, stumble across an alternate world where the Wild Hunt was never bound, and Darkbrook, the school of magic they attend, was abandoned a hundred years ago.

But when the Hounds of the Hunt wish to surrender, the two students are swept up in a whirlwind of heartbreak, betrayal, and the discovery of a lost treasure.

Publisher: http://www.writers-exchange.com/the-sixth-stone/

A Beth-Hill Novella: Karen Montgomery Series

Are creatures of the night and all manner of extramundane beings drawn to certain locations in the natural world? In the Midwestern village of Beth-Hill located in southern Ohio, the population is made up of its fair share of common citizens...and much more than its share of supernatural residents. Take a walk on the wild side in this unusual place where imagination meets reality.

Karen Montgomery was an ordinary woman until she stumbled into the extraordinary... A bargain with elves worth its weight in gold. A plague of sinister ladybugs. Rogue vampire hunters, including one who tries to turn over a new leaf--with disastrous consequences. A ghostly huntsmen of the Wild Hunt wishing for redemption. Karen's life will never be the same again.

Book 1: Budget Cuts

Karen Montgomery is used to taking care of the unpleasant jobs no one else wants to deal with. When a shortage of funds forces her to fire fifteen employees from the library, she isn't happy, but the nasty task has to be done and she is, after all, the boss. But Karen finds finishing her task impossible when she can't seem to track down Ivy Bedinghaus, a night clerk she's never actually met. Once she finally does confront Ivy, she's thrust into a centuries-old conflict that makes her previous troubles radically pale in comparison.
Publisher: http://www.writers-exchange.com/budget-cuts/

Book 2: The Secret of Redemption

Karen Montgomery, librarian, finds herself embroiled in another otherworldly adventure...

A member of the Wild Hunt--ghostly myths that aren't so ghostly (or myth-like) anymore--needs help in reconciling who he once was in life and who he is now.

A little girl has gone missing. And the one most likely responsible for her disappearance is the one Karen must prove innocent.
Publisher: http://www.writers-exchange.com/the-secret-of-redemption/

Book 3: Ladybug, Ladybug

An innocent attempt to rid the library of a plague of ladybugs turns sinister when a rogue vampire hunter gets the contract for pest control.

Ivy Bedinghaus, who works for Karen as a night clerk--along with all the vampires in Beth-Hill--are in danger, and their only hope for survival is with the help of Karen, a member of the Wild Hunt, and Russell Moore, a reformed vampire hunter.

Publisher: http://www.writers-exchange.com/ladybug-ladybug/

Book 4: Detour

One wrong turn sends Karen down a road that shouldn't exist, to the site of an old accident and an even older mystery. With reformed vampire hunter Russell Moore's help, Karen finds the key to the mystery. But Russ keeps his own secrets...some of which are deadly.

When old friends from Russ' past come to call, Karen realizes his secrets might just mean his doom. After a terrible incident three years ago, before Karen met him, Russ wants only to live the rest of his life quietly in Beth-Hill. But his secret might not allow him the new lease on life Russ longs for.

Publisher: http://www.writers-exchange.com/detour/

Companion Story: Russ' Story: Capture

Long before Russell Moore ever met supernatural sleuth Karen Montgomery or set foot in Beth-Hill, he was a vampire hunter, possibly the best vampire hunter of all. He brought down whole nests of vampires, caring little about the consequences of his actions. Anyone who lived with or helped the vampires became enemies to be slaughtered.

So what kind of an idiot would capture a ruthless vampire hunter without a conscience and try to reform him?

Ethan Walker was that idiot. Wanting to protect his family, Ethan set out to prove to Russ that vampires weren't all evil, soulless creatures. If Russ would allow himself to witness their lives, see their humanity, surely he and other vampire hunters like him would let them live in peace. *Surely?*

Publisher: http://www.writers-exchange.com/capture/

Secrets When in Shadow Lie

Twelve years ago, Ryan Grey was cursed by a witch to hide a secret. He's lived with the curse of being unable to die permanently, and, over the years he's slowly losing the memory of his past until almost nothing remains.

But now, after a chance meeting with an elf named Zipporah, he discovers the key to unlocking the secret and breaking the curse once and for all...if he can survive the breaking.

Publisher: http://www.writers-exchange.com/secrets-when-in-shadow-lie/

The Dead Who Do Not Sleep

Will Spark only wants a good night's sleep after a night of drinking. Instead, two thugs bang on his door, demanding answers to questions he can't understand. And then they killed him...

Publisher: http://www.writers-exchange.com/the-dead-who-do-not-sleep/

A Beth-Hill Novel: The Abby Duncan Series

Are creatures of the night and all manner of extramundane beings drawn to certain locations in the natural world? In the Midwestern village of Beth-Hill located in southern Ohio, the population is made up of its fair share of common citizens...and much more than its share of supernatural residents. Take a walk on the wild side in this unusual place where imagination meets reality.

Situated in Beth-Hill, where imagination meets reality, is The Rose Emporium, owned by elderly and not-a-little-odd Rose Duncan. The large Victorian house smackdab in the middle of nowhere is a cross between a pawn shop and an antique store that caters to supernatural creatures needing to barter. Rose's twenty-something niece, Abby Duncan, discovers that the world isn't made up of just run-of-the-mill, ordinary humans but an entire spectrum of unusual beings. With her preconceptions about what's normal and what's not turned upside-down, Abby is in for a whole lot of startling truths, mysteries-- about herself and the people and places around her--and danger.

Novella 1: By Any Other Name

Woodturner Abby Duncan decides to sell her spindles at a local Renaissance Festival with only some success. After all, no one really spins their own yarn anymore, do they? While there, she discovers that one of her newfound friends is not what he appears--and his secret is about to get him killed!

Publisher: http://www.writers-exchange.com/by-any-other-name/

Book 2: The Uncrowned Queen

Abby Duncan's elderly Aunt Rose has always been a bit odd. And now she's off on a mysterious trip, leaving Abby behind to run the Rose Emporium, an unusual sort of antique shop. Such an extraordinary store would have been a perfect place for Seth and the others, her friends from the Renaissance Festival, to take a break from traveling between Faires. But when tragedy strikes and Abby and the others discover the true nature of the Rose Emporium, they'll have to travel into Faerie itself before their tightknit group is whole again.

Abby doesn't know much about her family history, but she's about to find out the truth...whether she likes it or not.

Publisher: http://www.writers-exchange.com/the-uncrowned-queen/

Book 3: Coming Soon!

A Beth-Hill Novel: The Shadows Trilogy

Are creatures of the night and all manner of extramundane beings drawn to certain locations in the natural world? In the Midwestern village of Beth-Hill located in southern Ohio, the population is made up of its fair share of common citizens...and much more than its share of supernatural residents. Take a walk on the wild side in this unusual place where imagination meets reality.

A Dreamer dreams the future when the past is not yet laid to rest. Ten years ago, a plague swept across the Seven Kingdoms. Ten years ago, the Queen of Iomar's son was exiled and named the author of the magical plague. Now, in the present, Terrin works to complete his ultimate goal: Control of the Seven Kingdoms using his son's power to supplement his own. But his attempt at dominion meets resistance and the fate of the world rests in the unlikely hands of an exiled prince, a Dreamer, and a vampire...

Book 1: The Prince of Shadows

When Alban's father Terrin appeared at the castle door with a vampire in tow and apologies on his lips, Alban fell under his spell just like everyone else and welcomed him home. But Terrin didn't return to live quietly in his brother's kingdom. He had other plans and, with Alban's untrained powers at his disposal, he begins his ruthless plan to destroy the Seven Kingdoms and rule them all, beginning with his brother's death.

Terrin engineers events to cast the blame on his nephew, Teluride, intending to see the boy executed for his father's murder. But there are those who would thwart Terrin in his mad plan for power, and Alban forms an unlikely alliance with Skade, the reclusive Queen of Iomar, and Terrin's slave, a young vampire with no memory of his name or origins. Although the future looks grim, Alban and the vampire attempt to stop Terrin...and they almost succeed.

A darker history lies at the heart of Terrin's treachery, and only Skade knows the true reason why Terrin would murder his own brother and attempt to destroy both Alban and the vampire to achieve his goals. The Ghost who resides in Skade's mirror--her servant and thrall--holds one of the keys to Terrin's madness. Unfortunately, more than one person wishes for the past to remain the past and the future to hold no shadows of what might have been...

Publisher: http://www.writers-exchange.com/the-prince-of-shadows/

Book 2: Lost In Shadows

Events set in motion ten years ago come to a head as Skade, the reclusive Queen of Iomar, and Nicodemus, who is imprisoned by Skade, struggle to free Alban and the vampire from Terrin's grasp. Old secrets come to light when Skade's exiled son is forced to face his past--or die trying to redeem himself once and for all. Can the crimes of the past truly be forgiven? Only time will tell...and time is running out.

Publisher: http://www.writers-exchange.com/lost-in-shadows/

Book 3: Bound In Shadows

With his power crushed, brother to the king and father to Alban, Terrin is forced to take drastic measures to regain his sons after they are freed and harness the power they possess. But he has an ally inside the healer's house where they are recovering who works to further his plans. The Queen of Iomar, Skade's son, courts redemption to try to save his mother's life, and the vampire who no longer remembers his own name dreams a dream that might save them all...or damn them if success is thwarted.

Publisher: http://www.writers-exchange.com/bound-in-shadows/

A Beth-Hill Novel: Wild Hunt Series

Are creatures of the night and all manner of extramundane beings drawn to certain locations in the natural world? In the Midwestern village of Beth-Hill located in southern Ohio, the population is made up of its fair share of common citizens...and much more than its share of supernatural residents. Take a walk on the wild side in this unusual place where imagination meets reality.

The Wild Hunt roamed the forest outside of Beth-Hill until the Council bound them for a hundred years. Nevertheless, a century of existence has made an indelible mark not easily forgotten for these ghostly myths that are no longer so ghostly or myth-like...

Book 1: Heart's Desire

The Wild Hunt roamed the forest outside of Beth-Hill until the Council bound them for a hundred years--a lifetime for a human but only a passing thought to one such as Gabriel, Master of the Wild Hunt. As the Council's binding draws to a close, old enemies reappear to ensure that the Wild Hunt is bound once more--to a creature much worse than the Council has been.

Publisher: http://www.writers-exchange.com/hearts-desire/

Book 2: Fire and Water

As a young vampire, Erialas Morgan brought his mother back to life with a spell that shouldn't exist, shouldn't have worked...perhaps shouldn't have been performed at all. Desperation and love are his only excuses for doing the unthinkable.

There are others who wish to use that same spell for their own gain--and to destroy the Wild Hunt once and for all. Caught in the middle of a war between the Morgan clan of vampires and their human kin, Erialas turns to the Hunt for help. But even Gabriel, the Master of the Wild Hunt, may not be able to stop the tide of death and destruction once it turns.

Publisher: http://www.writers-exchange.com/fire-and-water/

Book 3: The Lost

Almost sixty years ago, Darkbrook, the only school of magic in the United States, opened its doors to students of decidedly different natures, sending out letters of invitation to the elves, the dragons, and the vampires. The three who responded to the invitation banded together despite their differences but vanished only weeks later along with an entire classroom full of students and their teacher after a field trip gone horribly wrong.

The Wild Hunt has healed and the Hounds have grown closer together, keeping Darkbrook's forest safe and secure for those who live there. Malachi, one of the eldest members of the Wild Hunt, has adapted to Josiah's spell to help him see, but when a demon boy trapped in the body of a human body for sixty years inside the school disrupts the newfound calm, the Hunt--and those they protect--are thrust into a struggle that should have ended long ago when a vampire, an elf, and a dragon vanished into the Mists.

Publisher: http://www.writers-exchange.com/the-lost/

Book 4: A Glint of Silver

Jericho is a vampire who wants is to live away from the Richmond household of vampires led by his ruthless father Connor. When Jericho tries to escape, Connor punishes him and leaves him to die. Tristan is determined to be the one to bring Jericho back, but he can't see him suffer for wanting a normal life. As long as Connor lives, Jericho will never be safe or free. As long as Connor *lives*...

Publisher: http://www.writers-exchange.com/a-glint-of-silver/

Book 5: All That Glitters

As a member of the cruel Morgan Household of vampires, twelve-year-old Arthur Morgan has been abused all his life.

Maya, a water fairy, shows him just how horrible and twisted the household he's grown up is. With her help, and the unexpected help of an adult vampire, Arthur attempts to escape.

Can he become something more than what his father has decreed?

Publisher: http://www.writers-exchange.com/all-that-glitters/

The Chelsea Chronicles

Normally a quiet, serene place, Chelsea Kingdom seems like the perfect location for a centuries' old vampire to blend in and live a normal life, even escape hunters and an angry mob. Unfortunately, his timing couldn't be worse...

Book 1: So You Want to be a Vampire

Chelsea Kingdom is usually a pretty quiet place but recent murders--committed by a vampire--upset the calm. Newcomer to town, Vlad Dhalgren wants only to blend in and live a normal life. He quickly learns that isn't possible, given that other vampires have been hiding in the shadows around the castle--in plain sight--for years.

Despite her lineage, Anna Everett, the crown princess of the Kingdom of Chelsea, isn't a wizard like her father, which means she will never be Queen. She has only one friend, Valerian Moreton--Val--who has secrets he's never shared that could get him *and* Anna killed...

Publisher: http://www.writers-exchange.com/so-you-want-to-be-a-vampire/

Book 2: Transformation

As Anna, crown princess of Chelsea, adjusts to life as a vampire after recent events, Vlad plans for a future he has no real hope to seeing come to pass due to injuries sustained while attempting to save Anna's life. But, as life goes on for Anna and her friend Valerian "Val" Moreton, it changes for others--some of whom are not quite what they seem...

Publisher: http://www.writers-exchange.com/transformation/

You can find ALL our books up on our website at:

http://www.writers-exchange.com

All Jennifer's books:

http://www.writers-exchange.com/Jennifer-St-Clair/

all our fantasy novels:

http://www.writers-exchange.com/category/genres/fantasy/

www.ingramcontent.com/pod-product-compliance
Lightning Source LLC
Chambersburg PA
CBHW052037150726
48002CB00002B/651